yolo

The Party Has Just Begun:

wtf

fml

yolo

Sam Jones

Simon Pulse
New York | London | Toronto | Sydney | New Delhi

SIMON PULSE
An imprint of Simon & Schuster Children's Publishing Division
1230 Avenue of the Americas, New York, NY 10020
First Simon Pulse paperback edition June 2014
Copyright © 2014 by Simon & Schuster, Inc.
Also available in a Simon Pulse hardcover edition
For information about special discounts for bulk purchases, please contact
Simon & Schuster Special Sales at 1-866-506-1949 or business@simonandschuster.com.
The Simon & Schuster Speakers Bureau can bring authors to your live event.
For more information or to book an event contact the Simon & Schuster Speakers Bureau
at 1-866-248-3049 or visit our website at www.simonspeakers.com.
Designed by Karina Granda
The text of this book was set in Tyfa ITC.
Manufactured in the United States of America
2 4 6 8 10 9 7 5 3 1
Library of Congress Control Number 2014936242
ISBN 978-1-4814-1549-1 (hc)
ISBN 978-1-4814-1548-4 (pb)
ISBN 978-1-4814-1550-7 (eBook)

To Jimmy Brooks

chapter 1

Emily O'Brien slipped behind the steering wheel of the late-model SUV her father had given her last year for her sixteenth birthday and turned the key in the ignition. She was relieved to see that the clock on the dash glowed exactly eleven a.m. Emily was not the type of person who enjoyed running behind schedule, nor was she the type of person who might frequently use the words "late-model SUV." Her father, however, did both of these things with alarming regularity.

But being late and using sort-of-douchey phrases to describe things was not the end of the world. Still, as she pulled out of the driveway and headed toward Ana's house, she was glad to have a break from her father's eccentricities. Just this morning while she'd been trying to get packed and out of the house, he was underfoot the entire time: in the kitchen blending a carrot-kale protein shake for breakfast, in the laundry room arranging his bike shorts on the drip-dry rack, in the hallway checking out his abs in the full-length mirror by the guest bath. Finally, she just pushed by him with her weekend bag.

"Oh! Sorry, sweetheart."

"Shouldn't you be working by now?" Emily asked.

"Self-employment, babe-EEE." He waggled the "hang loose" sign back and forth, his thumb and pinky stretched out. "Membership has its privileges."

Emily grimaced. "You're not a surfer, Dad."

Having a self-employed father is fine during the school year, she'd explained to her best friend, Ana Rodriguez. But now that junior year was finally over, the past few days felt like she'd been hanging out with a guy who'd stayed in college too long.

"Where you headed?" he asked.

"The Steins' party. Upstate. Remember?"

"Oh yeah! Par-TAY!"

Emily rubbed her temples. "Dad. Please. Don't."

"Text me when you get there, babe."

"Don't call me 'babe.'"

"Sorry, sweetie."

"Or sweetie."

"C'mon, Em! Lighten up! You're on your way to a fun weekend at that beautiful house in the mountains. Tell Mr. Stein I said 'WhassUUUUP?'"

"I will do no such thing." Emily sighed. "I will tell him you send your regards."

"Regards? *Regards?*" Her dad shook his head, laughing. "School's out, Em! Ditch the vocab quiz. Remember . . ."

"Don't!" Emily tried to cut him off, running for the door that lead into the garage from the kitchen, but it was too late.

"YOLO!" her dad had crowed as she fled with her bag. As Emily closed the door behind her, she heard him yell out the definition, as he always did: *You only live once!*

Emily turned up the volume on her new summer playlist, hoping to tune out the embarrassing sound of her father's voice echoing in her head. It was worse when he did this in front of her friends—and especially mortifying when he had done it in front of Kyle. Her father and Kyle had acted like stoned frat boys before she and Kyle called it quits. Kyle had been smoking way too much weed, and the thought of dating a total burnout the summer before senior year was more than Emily could take. Plus, she was tired of every man in her life telling her to "lighten up" and "take it easy."

The simple truth was that junior year had been *hard*. *You try to lighten up while taking AP chemistry*—that's what she wanted to tell her dad and Kyle. It was like running a gauntlet that never seemed to (a) end or (b) get any more interesting. It was hard enough to study difficult subjects, but chemistry was one of those academic situations Emily found so boring she could barely pay attention. Still, she had studied until she thought her eyeballs would melt and her brain would come sliding out of her right ear. She'd gotten an A-minus by a single percentage point on the final exam, but she'd had to sacrifice nearly every social engagement for the last two months of school to pull it off.

The only thing she hadn't ditched was prom, and Kyle got so drunk at the after party that he had barfed in her purse.

It was at that precise moment last month, standing by Ana's pool with a clutch full of Kyle's puke, that Emily had for once decided to take her father's cool dude advice: *Let go! Don't hold on so tight to every freaking thing.*

The thing she let go of first was Kyle.

Ana had helped her get Kyle into a cab, and then driven her home. After that, it was weird at school for the last month of classes. Kyle kept puppy-dogging her around campus, begging her to take him back. At first Emily was friendly but firm:

"Not going to happen, Kyle. I have a lot of cute purses. None of them are designed to carry vomit."

Then after a particularly trying week in which final projects were due in every class and she'd refereed yet another screaming match between Ana and her other best friend, Brandon, (this time over pizza toppings), she made the mistake of watching a movie on cable with Juliette Lewis and Giovanni Ribisi. They both played differently-abled young people who fell in love, and by the end, she was a puddle on the living room carpet. In a moment of weakness she'd texted Kyle to come over, and he'd appeared at her doorway in five minutes. He smelled like pot, but his smile made her knees weak. Emily's dad was already in bed, and they'd spent three hours on the couch together that night—only one of them with their clothes on.

At that point Kyle started acting like they were back together again: meeting Emily at her locker every day and texting a lot. For the past few weeks, he'd been begging her to "make it official" again. Emily was torn. People did change, after all. That much was clear when her mom had left a few years back. Frankly, she wasn't sure if it was fair to ask Kyle to change—especially since he was always telling her to "chillax." God, she hated that nonword hybrid. It made her skin crawl every time he said it. She was so tired of her focus being mocked, the subject of eye rolls and derision—especially from a cute stoner who couldn't even spell the word "derision," much less use it in a sentence.

See? There she was, looking down on Kyle again. And that was at the heart of her dilemma of whether to get back together with him again or not: respect. At the end of the day Emily was unsure that they had any respect for each other. In a way, she felt that they both wanted the other to be somebody different. On the flip side Emily didn't know if she had the strength to truly make things final with Kyle. He could be very persuasive, and so she'd taken the path of least resistance and just started ignoring his texts and phone calls. Her silence had only served to increase the frequency and intensity of Kyle's attempts to contact her. She'd received two more texts just in the time it had taken to get to Ana's neighborhood.

As she pulled into Ana's driveway, the clock on the dash read 11:07. Three minutes ahead of schedule. Emily's goal was to be pulling onto the highway at noon. The on-ramp was only five minutes from Ana's house, but Emily knew it would take a minimum of ten minutes just to get Ana focused enough to leave her front door the first time, and another five to seven minutes of trips back inside to procure forgotten items before Ana would finally strap on her seat belt. Plus, they had one additional stop to make.

The schedule was tight, but Emily smiled when she thought about this weekend and finally being on the road toward Jacob and Madison's big house in the mountains. The view from the infinity pool alone was worth the drive. One thing was certain: The twins knew how to throw a party. Jacob could DJ a complete meltdown into existence, spinning tracks that made the whole pool deck pulse like a beautiful wild animal with a biological imperative to bump and grind. Madison was the queen of convincing the sweetest, cutest college guys Emily had ever seen to wear as little as possible in the hot tub. What's more, Madison was never greedy or jealous, one of those rare pretty girls who isn't as crazy as she is pretty. She was all about spreading the wealth, literally and figuratively.

Emily smiled as the song ended. She jumped out of the car, the tune still bouncing in her step as she ran up the front-porch stairs and rang Ana's doorbell.

chapter 2

Ana Rodriguez did *chaîné* turns across the tile in her foyer, her long black hair flying around her head as she spotted the banister, then did a *grand jeté* leap onto the third stair and squealed like a banshee all the way up to her bedroom. Emily giggled in spite of herself as she followed.

"Oh my God, Ana. How can you do ballet with such a huge rack?"

Ana ran her hands across her tight black halter top, swiveling her hips seductively as she danced across the area rug in her bedroom toward Emily. "Years of practice, *mamacita. Mucho trabajo.*"

Ana pushed Emily down onto her bed, squealed again, then ran around throwing random items of clothing into two different leather bags. "I cannot believe that my parents are letting me go for the whole weekend!"

"Me neither," Emily said. "Did you tell them we're going to a party?"

"Yes."

"Hosted by the Steins?"

"Well, sort of." Ana's copper lips curled into a smirk.

Emily shook her head. "What did you tell your parents?"

"Just that we're going to the party. At the Steins'. For their church."

Emily blinked. "Their . . . *church?*"

"What?"

"Ana, their last name is *Stein.*"

"Yeah. So . . . ?"

"They're *Jewish.*"

Ana frowned. "That's okay, right?"

Emily shook her head. "Yes. It's fine. But they don't go to . . . church. Maybe a temple? I don't think the Steins are very . . . religious."

Ana threw herself across the bed. "I told my mom that they had committed their hearts to Jesus, and were hosting a benefit for the food bank at their church. I can tell them it was a temple later if they ask."

Emily smiled and shook her head at her best friend. Ana's parents were Catholics and attempted to keep their daughter on a tight leash. Nature had been working against them since the summer between seventh and eighth grade when Ana had been blessed with a body that made Jennifer Lopez look like a Sunday-school teacher.

"Are you almost ready?" Emily asked. "What can I do to help?"

"Nothing! I'm almost packed." Ana dumped an armful of heels into the second leather bag.

"Um, Ana? You do know that we're only going to be there for approximately thirty-six hours, right?"

Ana glanced down at the twelve pairs of shoes in the bag, then looked up at Emily and frowned. "You're right. I may need another pair." She spun around and practically dive-rolled into her closet. "Tell me the plan."

Emily checked the time on her phone. "Well, we have to leave here in eight minutes if we want to get on the road by noon."

"Will we have time to stop and get food? I'm starving."

"As long as we leave by noon," Emily confirmed. "I want to get there between five and six so that we have time to take a disco nap and shower before the party gets going."

Ana squealed, emerging from the closet with two red sequined stilettos held over her head like the Holy Grail. "Look! Party pumps!" She slid her feet into them, and bouncy-dancing Ana suddenly became all legs and poise, the red pointy toes flashing a hint of sparkle from beneath the hem of her skinny jeans.

"Will your feet survive if you wear those?" Emily asked.

In reply, Ana kicked one leg up by her ear and held it there, balancing like a showgirl on the Vegas strip. "*Ay, mamacita.* My feet will be fine. The question is, will anyone else survive if I wear these?"

Emily smiled. Her friend had a point. These were shoes that might kill a man at twenty paces.

Ana laughed and clicked her red heels together like Dorothy. "There's no place like home."

"Let's go!" Emily grabbed the bag of shoes and zipped it up. "If I don't get you into the car, we'll never make it to Oz."

After one trip back in to get Ana's purse and another to fetch her sunglasses, Emily was certain that they could finally leave, when Ana suddenly bolted from the car one last time. She returned moments later with a brown paper grocery bag that she tossed into Emily's back seat with a clank.

"What was that?" Emily asked.

"Canned goods."

"Canned goods?"

"You know, for the food pantry," Ana said, buckling her seat belt.

Emily shook her head. "Your mom left you with a bag of canned goods for the Steins' 'church'?"

Ana shrugged and grinned. "You only live once."

chapter 3

Emily held her breath and kept her eyes on the road as she made a right turn a few blocks before the freeway on-ramp. Ana was making a playlist on her phone while doing her patented brand of seat dancing, and talking through the pros and cons of a bikini versus a one-piece swimsuit for later tonight in the Steins' hot tub.

Maybe she won't notice, Emily thought.

Naturally, at that exact moment Ana stopped midsentence. "Hey . . ." Her voice trailed off. "Where are you going?"

Emily braced her hands against the leather of the steering wheel, and in her brightest you're-going-to-*love*-this voice said, "One last stop!" From the corner of her eye, she saw a shadow cross Ana's face as she peered at the houses on this residential street, then whirled back toward Emily.

"Oh, *hell no*."

"What?" Emily started to panic, but this was the moment of truth.

"Don't you play stupid with me. You are a double-crossing *gringa* and you know it." Ana started pulling her bags out of the back seat. "You need to stop this car and let me out right here."

Emily sped up slightly. She could see Brandon's house. Third down on the left. She knew Ana hadn't spoken to Brandon since they'd broken up at the beginning of school last fall. It had been awkward for everyone for the past nine months, and Emily had to admit that this was the shadiest part of her plan for the perfect weekend. She was taking a calculated risk.

Emily had known Brandon since they were six years old, when he moved in next door to her. She'd known the feisty Latina girl in the passenger seat would be their third musketeer the moment Ana pirouetted into Brandon with a full tray of spaghetti on the first day of seventh grade. She'd also known it would be an unmitigated disaster when Ana and Brandon announced they were going out at the beginning of sophomore year.

Emily had begged and pleaded. She'd actually prayed. On her knees. To the capital G God her grandmother believed in. All of this was to no avail. Emily knew the googly eyes of August would turn into stress over commitment when it was time to pick out Christmas presents. She knew that Ana would drive Brandon one kind of crazy in the backseat of his car, and a different kind of crazy in the front seat. This was oil and water, and there was no way the two of them would mix, but that wasn't the chemistry about which Ana and Brandon were concerned. They had kissed under the Labor Day fireworks in the park at the beginning of sophomore year, but by the time Valentine's Day rolled around, the explosive on-again/off-again nature of things was taking its toll.

By the time Ana and Brandon had broken up over July Fourth weekend last summer, Emily had learned to hang out with them separately. She was Switzerland, the neutral party, the no-man's-land, the friend happily yodeling with her fingers in her ears while she waited for them to finally make up.

Until today.

Today Emily couldn't take it any longer. She wanted both Ana and Brandon at this party. After a school year of stress at being pulled back and forth between them, and homework, and Kyle, and her dad's midlife crisis, she was done playing it safe.

She knew both of them wanted to be at this party.

She knew both of them loved her.

She knew that if she could make it to Brandon's driveway, and he was waiting on the steps as she'd asked him to do, that Ana would be too mortified to get out of the car.

Emily popped into Brandon's driveway a little too hot and screeched to a stop. He was waiting for them on the porch, according to plan, waving like a little kid at a parade. "Don't be mad!" she said to Ana. It came out as more of a command than a plea.

Ana snorted. "Mad? Oh please. Mad does not begin to express the rage that I feel at this moment."

Brandon loped down the stairs, his backpack slung over his shoulder. He swept his shaggy brown bangs out of his eyes, and told Emily to pop the trunk.

He tossed in his backpack, closed the trunk, then slid his lanky frame into the backseat, and reached over to close the door. Ana had sunk so far down in her seat she was at eye level with the glove compartment. She was muttering words in Spanish that Emily was not familiar with, but they sounded scary.

Emily didn't wait for Brandon to close the door. She backed out of the driveway and sped toward the freeway. She knew, or maybe just hoped, that Ana would hesitate to kill her if the car was in motion.

"Whoa! Head's up, speed demon," Brandon said as he buckled his seat belt. "We in a hurry?"

Emily glanced at the clock. 11:55. "Nope!" she said. "We're right on schedule."

"Are you trying to tell me that I am going to be trapped in a car for the next four-and-a-half hours with this *pendejo*?" Ana was spitting her words like a machine gun.

"It might be closer to six hours, depending on how long we stop for lunch," Emily said sheepishly.

The sound Ana made in response was not pleasant, but she didn't throw herself from the moving car, so Emily decided to call it a win.

"Lunch sounds good," Brandon piped up from the backseat. "I could use a couple burgers."

"You could use a good kick in the nuts," Ana muttered.

Something snapped inside of Emily, and she pulled over to the curb and slammed on the breaks. Their seat belts almost cut them in half.

"ENOUGH." Emily's voice was like a foghorn. Ana's eyes

went wide, but her mouth stayed closed. Emily put the car in park and turned in her seat. "I can't handle it anymore. I was the one who said this would be a disaster from the beginning, but no one would listen to me. And I was right."

Ana flipped her hair over her shoulder. "But—"

"But nothing!" Emily grabbed Ana's knee and squeezed. "Did *you* listen to me when I said 'Don't start dating Brandon because it will ruin everything'?"

Ana shook her head. Emily turned to Brandon in the backseat.

"And you! Did *you* listen to me when I said, 'Don't start dating Ana because it will ruin everything'?"

Brandon held up both hands in surrender. "She beguiled me with her feminine charms. Evil woman witchcraft."

"Aaaaargh!" Ana clenched her fists and shook them in the air. "Em, why are you *doing this to me?*"

"This isn't something I'm doing to you, it's something you're doing to me," Emily said. "I've had to put up with both of you this whole year since you broke up. Besides being a huge pain in my ass emotionally, it has been a scheduling *nightmare*. I'm done. I've had it. I want both of you at this party. I want both of you to ride up with me. After what I've dealt with for the past nine months, the two of you can deal with it for the next six hours."

Suddenly, unexpectedly, there were tears in Emily's eyes, and she whirled back to face the windshield. But it was too late. Ana caught a glimpse and reached out to put a hand on her arm.

"I just want my friends back," Emily said, brushing her tears away before they could make her mascara run. "Is that too much to ask?"

Ana glanced into the backseat at Brandon, who shot her the mischievous grin that had won her over in an instant, then tormented her for a year. She sighed and turned back to Emily. "I'll do my best, but only because I love you and you're my best friend. Just as long as he leaves me alone."

Emily adjusted the rearview mirror so she could see Brandon. "Brandon? Can you handle that?"

Brandon smirked at her in the mirror. "Yeah, sure. I can handle that."

Ana turned up the music. Emily put the car in drive, merged into traffic, then made a quick right turn. As she pulled up the on-ramp onto the highway, the clock on the dash flipped from 11:59 to 12:00, and she smiled. Finally, they were on the right track. Ana must have felt it too, because she began dancing right there in the front seat, and then Brandon was singing at the top of his lungs, and as Emily merged into traffic she couldn't help singing along. The tension of the past few minutes, and the past few months, started to melt away from her neck and shoulders. The worst was over, and Emily knew it'd be nothing but a good time for the rest of the weekend.

chapter 4

"Oh my God. Why are you doing that to us?"

"What?" Emily turned down the volume just a little.

"Singing Pink like Julie Andrews."

Brandon snort-laughed in the backseat.

"Shut up!" Emily slapped at Ana's leg, but she couldn't help giggling. They'd been on the road for an hour now. The suburbs had gradually receded into the distance, and now they just had open road ahead of them. With the release of all the tension from before, things had been nothing but great, and now it seemed Brandon and Ana were even starting to get along, if Brandon's continued laughter was any indication. "You two are supposed to hate each other," Emily said, "not gang up and hate on me."

"*Pobrecita.*" Ana rubbed the tip of her thumb and forefinger together. "This is the world's smallest violin playing 'Cry Me a River.'"

Brandon's head popped between the front seats. "Hey, speaking of violins, remember that chick from NYU who came to the Steins' Labor Day party and got so wasted she took her violin into the hot tub and played 'Flight of the Bumblebee'?"

"She was a train wreck," Ana said.

"True," said Emily, "but she had surprisingly good technique."

"Hope she's back again this time." Brandon sighed. "I could use a little technique myself."

Emily groaned while Ana spun in her seat. "That! That right there."

"What?" Brandon sounded surprised, but Emily could hear the smirk in his voice. He loved egging Ana on.

"You are such a pig," Ana huffed.

"Wait, what? How am I a pig because I want to make out with a hot girl?"

"I'm right HERE." Ana shook her head.

"And I'd make out with you if you still wanted to," said Brandon. "You're the one who broke up with me, remember?"

"Because of crap like *that*," Ana said. "We were still together at that Labor Day party, and your tongue was hanging so far out of your mouth, it's a wonder you didn't trip on it and break your neck."

"So what?" Brandon said. "We were *dating*, not *dead*. So I wasn't supposed to notice when there are other hot girls around just because I was going out with you?"

Emily sighed. "Guys. You're doing it again." Brandon and Ana both started talking at the same time, and Emily decided to use her considerable vocal power to put her proverbial foot down. She switched off the radio and shouted, "GUYS!"

Ana and Brandon flopped back against their respective seats.

"Thank you," Emily said. "Look, Brandon, I think what Ana means is that *of course* you're going to notice other girls, but that she wants to be the one you notice the most. It's one thing to see other hot girls. It's another thing to pay so much attention to them that your girlfriend feels ignored."

"*Exactly* what I was trying to say," Ana chimed in.

Emily held up her hand to silence her friend. "And, Ana, what *Brandon* is saying, is that he was there at the party with *you*, and that he wanted you to trust him and feel secure enough in your relationship that you didn't care if he noticed some other hot girl, because you know you're hot just the way you are. Insecurity is never sexy."

"*Totally*," Brandon said from the backseat. "How did you do that?"

"Do what?" Emily glanced at Brandon in the rearview mirror.

"Sum up what both of us were saying like you're some sort of freakin' psychologist?"

Emily smiled. "I just pay attention to both of you. I love you guys. You're my friends. It's the reason I didn't think you would ever work as a couple: You would both be so worried about losing the other one that you'd never actually do the simple things you're supposed to do to make sure that doesn't happen. Like listen to each other."

They drove in silence for a little while. Emily knew she'd probably hit a nerve with both of her friends, since she'd never explicitly stated why she thought they shouldn't date.

But now it was out there, and they could think about that for a while. She didn't mind the silence. She'd liked the easy-going attitude they'd had just a few minutes before, but the silence was more welcome than the incessant arguing that was bound to happen otherwise. And out here on the highway, there was only the rumbling monotone of car tires speeding down the pavement road. The forest around them was just starting to transform into open farmland, and the sun was shining, and they were making great time. If this was going to be the trip, Emily had little to complain about.

"Sooo," Ana said slowly, extending the word as she turned in her seat to face Emily. "Who do you want to meet at the party?"

Emily blinked. "Me? Meet?"

"Yeah," Brandon chimed in. "What's your best case scenario for this weekend?"

"I have zero expectations," Emily said. "I just want to have a good time."

"Bullshit, *mamacita*." Ana was having none of it. "You don't fool me. Not one little bit."

"What?" Emily put on her wide-eyed innocent look, but Brandon wasn't buying either.

"Oh, c'mon." Brandon let out an exaggerated sign. "There it is. The trademark Emily O'Brian big eyes of I-don't-know-what-you-mean. Dead giveaway."

"A dead giveaway for *what*?" Emily was blushing now, her voice floating up a couple of octaves toward squeak territory.

"A dead giveaway that you have a plan," Ana said, narrowing her eyes. "In fact, you know *exactly* what you're looking for at this party, don't you?"

Emily kept both eyes forward. "I will not stand for these wild allegations."

"Oh, gimme a break," Brandon shot back. "You've already got him imagined right down to the skinny jeans and the Columbia student ID. You're looking for pre-med—"

"Or pre-law," Ana cut in, "and a loft in Tribeca that Daddy bought when he was in junior high to make sure he didn't have to live in the dorm."

"Ooh, good one," Brandon held up a high five which Ana smacked, much to Emily's amazement.

"See?" Emily said. "The two of you are never more united than when your purpose is to make me miserable."

"Don't try to change the subject," Brandon said. "I bet you're looking for one of those poor little rich boys who *wishes* he lived over in Williamsburg, but he's decided to tough it out in Tribeca and just grow a beard in solidarity." Brandon was laughing so hard he could barely finish painting this picture.

"A beard? Ew."

"Oh please. Ew all you want. You are so easy to peg," Ana said, twisting a strand of her hair around her fingers. "It's like shooting fish in a barrel."

"What makes you think *that's* what I'd be looking for?"

"You have a type." Brandon announced this as if he were

stating that the sky was, indeed, blue. "You love a rich pretty boy with a broken heart and a bank account. You like 'em complicated."

"Kyle wasn't complicated," Emily protested.

"Exactly," said Ana. "And look how that ended up?"

"Don't make me pull this car over," Emily growled.

"I wish you would," said Brandon. "I'm starving."

"Well, you should have thought about that before you started openly mocking the driver." Emily shot an evil grin at Brandon.

"C'mon, Em, I'm so hungry," Brandon pleaded.

"Don't call me 'Em.' And stop begging. It's not cute."

"Well, it *can* be . . ." Ana said under her breath but still loud enough for Emily to hear.

"What?" Emily's jaw dropped open.

"Nothing," Ana said quickly, though she was smiling as she remembered something.

"When did you make Brandon beg?" Emily demanded. "Tell me. Now."

"Beg? I never begged," Brandon said loudly.

"Keep clinging to that raft, big guy." Ana had a spark in her eye.

"Spill it," said Emily.

"Let's just say, I can make this one squirm," Ana told Emily, jabbing a thumb in Brandon's direction.

"Whatever!" Brandon howled in the backseat. "I'd never give you the satisfaction."

"Likewise," Ana told Emily. "Why do you think he was squirming?"

"Foul!" Brandon yelled.

Emily was laughing. Ana giving Brandon a hard time was definitely better than Ana and Brandon giving *her* a hard time. This is what she loved most about having these two as her best friends: No one was going to let anyone get away with anything. She could totally be herself.

"I'll have both of you know that I am certainly *not* looking for a college boy," Emily announced. "Or an heir. I'm not looking for anything really. Just a good time."

"Yeah, a good time named Trenton Percival Howell III," teased Brandon.

"Wearing Ray-Bans," giggled Ana.

Even Emily had to laugh at this. "Ray-Bans?" she asked. "Really? My type is so particular he has specific sunglasses?"

"And underwear," Brandon said. "Calvin Klein boxer briefs."

"Totally!" Ana was laughing so hard she had tears running down her cheeks.

"Don't make me pull this car over." Emily tried to sound like an angry dad on a TV show, but this just made Ana laugh harder. "I'll pull it over and kick you guys out and leave you there."

"For the love of God, if you do pull the car over and leave us on the side of the road, *please* do it near some kind of rest stop because I'm *starving*. My stomach is literally eating itself." Brandon curled up in the backseat and groaned.

"We're kind of in the middle of nowhere," Emily said as she looked around.

"So is that place." Ana pointed at an old and tattered billboard as they passed under it. RICK'S DINER: BREAKFAST, LUNCH, AND DINNER. OPEN 24-HOURS. HOME OF THE STRAWBERRY TSUNAMI.

"What the hell is a Strawberry Tsunami?" Brandon wondered aloud.

"Only one way to find out," Emily said. She put on her blinker and merged into the right-hand lane. She hadn't realized until Ana pointed out the sign, but she was actually pretty hungry herself.

"Ugh. What am I going to find to eat at Rick's Diner that is on my diet?" Ana whined.

"You said you were hungry when we left your house," Emily reminded her. "And you're the one who pointed out the billboard. The better question is why the hell are you on a diet at all?" Ana was constantly complaining about her ass being too big. She was curvy, but not a single pound overweight.

"Yeah," said Brandon. "You're always talking about how you're on a diet, but you always look great."

Ana sighed and slumped in her seat. "I'm sure they have some sort of salad."

"And *I'm* sure that you are not leaving that diner until you eat an onion ring with me." Emily was tired of this nonsense. She turned on the music, which happened to be Beyoncé, and sang along. *"All the single ladies..."*

Brandon joined in, complete with choreography. Soon

"Yes," said Ana, staring in horror at the tabletop. "I'll need stretcher and an ambulance to carry my friends away once hey eat themselves into a diabetic coma."

The waitress laughed, and Brandon and Ana began snapping pictures of the plates one at a time. Emily spread mayo nd ketchup on her burger, and was hefting the whole thing o her mouth when Ana smacked her arm. "Hang on. I need a icture of this."

Emily bit down on the burger like she was in a commercial n TV and Ana squealed as she snapped the shot. "That is the erfect summer image." She swiped and tapped a couple of imes as she uploaded the shot to Instagram, just as Brandon agged Emily on Facebook in the same shot from his side of he table.

"Okay, you two," Emily said as she swallowed the delicious first bite. "Enough with documenting the food. Eat it!" She forked two onions rings onto Ana's bowl of salad, and watched as Ana tentatively put one in her mouth.

"Oh. My. *God*." Ana sighed as she chewed. "This is the best thing that has ever been fried in hot oil."

After two more bites of the cheeseburger, Emily passed it off to Brandon and tried a bite of his Reuben before doing what might have been described as a face plant in the grilled cheese. As she was dipping a chicken finger in honey mustard, the waitress reappeared just in time with a handful of fresh napkins.

"I don't know how you do it," she said as Emily grabbed

Ana was laughing as they pulled off the highway at the exit for Rick's Diner, which was just off the side of the road. As Emily pulled into a parking spot, Ana sighed.

"Fine," she said. "One onion ring. But only one."

"And a Strawberry Tsunami," Emily shouted.

"Absolutely not," Ana said, shaking her head violently. "You can't make me."

"Hashtag YOLO," said Brandon. "I've gotta take a whiz." Then he jumped out of the car and ran into the restaurant.

chapter 5

The diner looked like something from the set of a high school theater production of *Grease*. There were red vinyl booths with metallic flecks in the plastic. Every table had a Formica top with curved chrome trim. There was a jukebox playing oldies in the corner, and a counter crammed with truckers, travelers, and teenagers. And the neon lights that ran along the top of the walls glowed bright red, pink, and radioactive green.

After Emily and Ana walked in, they were quickly seated at a booth by a waitress wearing a pink-striped jumper, glasses on a chain around her neck, and a bouffant hairdo a color of orange that nature never intended. Emily slid in next to the window, and Ana sat next to her. Seconds later, Brandon slid into the other side and let out a low whistle.

"Can you believe this place?" he asked with a grin. "Go, greased lightning."

"Right?" said Emily. "I want a double cheeseburger right this second."

She flipped open her menu as Ana and Brandon did the same. Ana let out a gasp. "Holy cow! There must be twenty-

seven pages in this menu. They have every sandwich y[ou] possibly imagine."

"And a few that you can't . . ." Brandon pointed to [a] thing called a "tongue" sandwich. "How 'bout we *not* or[der one] of those."

"Agreed," said Emily and Ana said together.

Emily ordered food like she'd been stoned for a [week] and was finally going to satisfy her munchies once and [for all]. Brandon joined in. By the time the waitress left thei[r table,] Ana was shaking her head in disbelief.

"How are we *possibly* going to eat all of that food?"

"We're not," said Emily. "But I *am* going to try a [bit of] everything."

"And I plan to finish whatever she doesn't," said B[randon.]

"And don't forget," Emily said, "we have to save ro[om for] Strawberry Tsunami."

"*A* Strawberry Tsunami?" asked Brandon. He sh[ook his] head. "I'll be having one of those on my own, so you'[ll want to] plan to order one for yourself."

The waitress brought the food out in shifts. Firs[t the] tuna salad on field greens arrived with Emily's double [cheese-] burger and onion rings, and Brandon's pastrami Reul[en and] french fries. The stuffed grilled cheese with bacon and t[omato] arrived next, along with a basket of chicken fingers an[d sweet] potato fries with extra ranch and honey-mustard dippi[ng sauce.]

"Is there anything else I can get you right now?" the [waitress] asked.

Ana was laughing as they pulled off the highway at the exit for Rick's Diner, which was just off the side of the road. As Emily pulled into a parking spot, Ana sighed.

"Fine," she said. "One onion ring. But only one."

"And a Strawberry Tsunami," Emily shouted.

"Absolutely not," Ana said, shaking her head violently. "You can't make me."

"Hashtag YOLO," said Brandon. "I've gotta take a whiz." Then he jumped out of the car and ran into the restaurant.

chapter 5

The diner looked like something from the set of a high school theater production of *Grease*. There were red vinyl booths with metallic flecks in the plastic. Every table had a Formica top with curved chrome trim. There was a jukebox playing oldies in the corner, and a counter crammed with truckers, travelers, and teenagers. And the neon lights that ran along the top of the walls glowed bright red, pink, and radioactive green.

After Emily and Ana walked in, they were quickly seated at a booth by a waitress wearing a pink-striped jumper, glasses on a chain around her neck, and a bouffant hairdo a color of orange that nature never intended. Emily slid in next to the window, and Ana sat next to her. Seconds later, Brandon slid into the other side and let out a low whistle.

"Can you believe this place?" he asked with a grin. "Go, greased lightning."

"Right?" said Emily. "I want a double cheeseburger right this second."

She flipped open her menu as Ana and Brandon did the same. Ana let out a gasp. "Holy cow! There must be twenty-seven pages in this menu. They have every sandwich you can possibly imagine."

"And a few that you can't . . ." Brandon pointed to something called a "tongue" sandwich. "How 'bout we *not* order one of those."

"Agreed," said Emily and Ana said together.

Emily ordered food like she'd been stoned for a month and was finally going to satisfy her munchies once and for all. Brandon joined in. By the time the waitress left their table, Ana was shaking her head in disbelief.

"How are we *possibly* going to eat all of that food?"

"We're not," said Emily. "But I *am* going to try a bite of everything."

"And I plan to finish whatever she doesn't," said Brandon.

"And don't forget," Emily said, "we have to save room for a Strawberry Tsunami."

"*A* Strawberry Tsunami?" asked Brandon. He shook his head. "I'll be having one of those on my own, so you'd better plan to order one for yourself."

The waitress brought the food out in shifts. First, Ana's tuna salad on field greens arrived with Emily's double cheeseburger and onion rings, and Brandon's pastrami Reuben with french fries. The stuffed grilled cheese with bacon and tomatoes arrived next, along with a basket of chicken fingers and sweet-potato fries with extra ranch and honey-mustard dipping sauce.

"Is there anything else I can get you right now?" the waitress asked.

"Yes," said Ana, staring in horror at the tabletop. "I'll need a stretcher and an ambulance to carry my friends away once they eat themselves into a diabetic coma."

The waitress laughed, and Brandon and Ana began snapping pictures of the plates one at a time. Emily spread mayo and ketchup on her burger, and was hefting the whole thing to her mouth when Ana smacked her arm. "Hang on. I need a picture of this."

Emily bit down on the burger like she was in a commercial on TV and Ana squealed as she snapped the shot. "That is the *perfect* summer image." She swiped and tapped a couple of times as she uploaded the shot to Instagram, just as Brandon tagged Emily on Facebook in the same shot from his side of the table.

"Okay, you two," Emily said as she swallowed the delicious first bite. "Enough with documenting the food. Eat it!" She forked two onions rings onto Ana's bowl of salad, and watched as Ana tentatively put one in her mouth.

"Oh. My. *God*." Ana sighed as she chewed. "This is the best thing that has ever been fried in hot oil."

After two more bites of the cheeseburger, Emily passed it off to Brandon and tried a bite of his Reuben before doing what might have been described as a face plant in the grilled cheese. As she was dipping a chicken finger in honey mustard, the waitress reappeared just in time with a handful of fresh napkins.

"I don't know how you do it," she said as Emily grabbed

the napkins and headed off a honey-mustard disaster in the area of her own chin.

"Do what?" Ana asked.

"Eat like that and keep those cute little figures," said the waitress.

"That's the point," Emily said, smiling. "We *don't* eat like this most of the time. We just got out of school this week, so we're sort of celebrating."

"Well, good for you." The waitressed grinned. "Lordy, I think I've gained ten pounds just standing here watching."

All three of them laughed as they watched the waitress waddle back to the kitchen. A few minutes later, and several more bites into the meal, Emily's phone buzzed. She wiped her hands, then grabbed it to check her messages.

First she saw all the alerts from their Instagrams, tweets, and, of course, the Facebook notification for the photo of her stuffing the cheeseburger into her mouth. It was already racking up the likes. "Nice," she said, nodding, as she showed Brandon and Ana. "I shall henceforth be known as Burger Girl."

She stopped short, staring at the screen after the last of her alerts had loaded. There, listed in the dropdown from the top of the screen, was an e-mail from Kyle. Just seeing his name reminded her that the last time she'd cut loose like this in a burger joint was at the mall not far from her house. It was the week before prom and Kyle had dragged her away from her chemistry textbook for exactly forty-five minutes. Something about the memory of his blue eyes staring at her over the chocolate malt they'd shared after their meal sent a wave of—what was it? Nostalgia? Pity?—over her. She couldn't decide if she missed Kyle, or if she just missed sharing a moment like this with someone who was more than a friend.

Her thumb hovered over the new message with Kyle's name in her in-box. Should she see what it said? Part of her was curious. The other part knew it was just him asking her to go out with him again. Did she want that? He kept messaging her saying that he had changed. But how much could one person change in one month? And even if Kyle had changed, was he the guy for her? Emily remembered the relief of finally making the decision to end things. She'd hardly looked back. Kyle wasn't a bad guy. He just wasn't *her* guy.

"Earth to Emily. Come in, Emily. Over." Brandon's voice broke into her thoughts, and she looked up to see both him and Ana staring at her.

Emily felt her cheeks flush. "What?"

"What's up with your phone?" Ana asked. "How can you be more interested in whatever is happening there than what is happening with these sweet-potato fries?" Emily laughed as Ana shoved aside her picked-over tuna salad plate and replaced it with the basket of golden-orange fries. She crammed four into her mouth after swiping them through the ranch dressing.

"Sorry," Emily said. She clicked the button and her phone screen went dark, then she dropped it back into her purse. "Hey, Brandon?"

"Yeah?" Brandon asked around a final ginormous bite of cheeseburger.

"Do you know . . ." Emily's voice trailed off. She didn't even want to put the question into words.

"Do I know what?" Brandon asked. He was now making short work of the grilled cheese that was left.

"Oh . . . nothing." Emily took a sip of her Coke and popped an onion ring into her mouth.

"Jesus. Why do girls always do that?" Brandon asked.

"Um, girls don't *always* do *anything*, thank you very much." Ana actually snapped her finger when she said this. "We are all individual creations of grace, beauty, and kick-ass-ness."

"Kick-ass-ness?" Brandon asked.

Ana nodded. "You heard me."

"Yeah. I also heard your friend with the blond hair and the onion-ring addiction just start to ask a question and not finish it." Brandon's eyes narrowed as he munched a couple of fries drenched in so much ketchup that they looked more like a glob of red than deep-fried potatoes.

"It was nothing," she said. "I . . . forgot what I was going to say."

"Uh-huh." Brandon wasn't buying it. "You know who I've *never ever in my life* heard start a question and then say 'Oh . . . nothing', Ana? A dude. That's who. Never once. And I know a lotta dudes."

Ana stuck out her tongue, which made Emily giggle and Brandon roll his eyes. "No thanks," he said. "I don't French long distance."

Ana groaned and threw a napkin at him. "You're such a pig. Spill it Emily. What were you going to ask him?"

Emily turned to look at her friend. This was so stupid. "I was just . . ."

"Spit it out," Brandon said, "or I'm gonna tell our waitress to eighty-six your Strawberry Tsunami."

Emily sighed. "Fine! Fine. I was going to ask you if Kyle was coming to the party."

Ana groaned. "Why would you care?"

"I know, I know. I shouldn't. It's just . . . well . . . he just e-mailed me, and I haven't talked to him at all since school got out, and I was just curious if I should worry that he's going to follow me around the party tonight."

"Why don't you read the message if you want to know if he's coming?" Brandon asked her. "I haven't heard from the dude since last week at school."

"And he wasn't coming?" Emily asked.

"Not that I know of." Brandon shrugged. "I mean, Em, either ignore him or don't, but if you're not going to read his messages, you have to be prepared that he might show up to the party."

Emily didn't want to talk about this anymore. She knew Brandon was right, and she felt like an idiot for bringing it up to begin with. So, when she saw the waitress headed back to the kitchen with an empty plate, Emily waved her down.

Surveying the table, the waitress sighed. "It looks like a great battle was fought at this booth."

"The onion rings won," groaned Ana. "I'm so full, I think I'm going to pop."

"To-go boxes for any of this?" the waitress asked.

"No, thank you," said Brandon politely. "We're actually headed to a party after this."

"Alrighty then. I'll be right back with your check."

"Actually," said Emily, "I was wondering . . ."

"Yes?" The waitress raised her eyebrows, obviously shocked that this thin girl with the blond hair might be ordering something more.

"Tell me about dessert," Emily said.

The waitress grinned and nodded, as if this were her goal from the beginning. "Now you're talking," she said. "Let me grab the dessert menu, and I'll be right back to tell you about your options."

chapter 6

When she returned, the waitress was carrying a menu that was larger than the one they'd seen with the appetizers and entrees, and seemed to feature a single dessert on each page, displayed in high-definition vibrant color on glossy paper. As the waitress flipped through the pages, Emily's eyes focused on only one thing: a giant parfait glass filled with what appeared to be a pink milkshake of epic proportions. She glanced at Brandon and saw from the look in his eyes that he'd noticed the page too. It was as if he were a caveman seeing a spark of fire for the very first time.

The waitress had stopped flipping to give her spiel about the Atomic Chocolate Brownie Bowl and the Apple Pie à la Explode on the opposite page, when Emily held up her hand, silently letting her know to stop.

"We're interested in the Strawberry Tsunami," she said.

The waitress's smile widened as she turned back a page to the pink dessert, which seemed to glow with some sort of inner light on the page.

"Is that the Strawberry Tsunami?" Emily queried.

Brandon's eyes were glazed over. "The one from the sign on the highway?"

"That's the one," the waitress said. "Three scoops of home-made strawberry ice cream and a piece of fresh strawberry pie—crust and all—blended to perfection, then layered into our biggest parfait glass with strawberry compote and more whipped cream than federal law should allow. Whatcha think?"

"Bring us one of those and three straws, please," Ana chirped. Brandon and Emily both turned to look at her, then slowly turned back to the waitress.

"Oh no," Emily said. "Bring us three of those with one straw apiece."

"What?!" Ana shrieked. "I am not drinking a whole one of those things. That's more calories than I'm supposed to eat in an entire day. It's more calories than *anyone* is supposed to eat in an entire day! I'll just have a sip of yours."

"I'm not sharing it," Emily said, shaking her head. "I haven't had a strawberry milkshake for at least two years, and I can't really say when it will happen again. I'm planning to drink every drop of that Tsunami or die trying."

Ana rolled her eyes and turned to Brandon. "Can't I just have a sip of yours?"

Brandon pointed at Emily. "What she said."

"Ugh." Ana flopped back against the booth and sighed. "Fine," she said. "Bring us three of them. But I'll need a to-go cup for mine."

The waitress laughed. "Comin' right up."

Emily checked her watch and smiled. "Right on time," she said, happily.

"Does it really matter if we're a few minutes later than we thought we'd be?" Brandon asked.

Emily simply winked in his direction. Brandon had never understood the simple pleasure it brought her to know that all things were going according to plan. A place for everything, and everything in its place; this was a rule that applied not only to closets and sock drawers, but also to schedules—especially important schedules. And what could be more important than this party? When things were on schedule, that meant nothing was going wrong. And when nothing went wrong, that meant the maximum relaxation time. When relaxation time is limited, getting the most possible is crucial.

Ana was staring out the window, eyeing a couple of diners who had just walked by. Emily followed her gaze and saw the pair from behind as they made their way to the door. The guy was short and stocky and was wearing combat boots with red track pants and a hooded sweatshirt with the sleeves cut off. Both of his arms were fully covered in tattoos, and the biceps that bulged when he held open the door looked like something from a comic book superhero. Or villain—Emily couldn't decide.

"Like what you see, *mamacita*?" Ana nudged Emily in the ribs, and Emily immediately blushed and turned away.

"What is he wearing?" she whispered.

"I don't know," said Ana. "Some sort of grunge garage-sale chic. Don't stare too long though. He's not headed to Harvard."

Brandon laughed. He'd turned around to catch a glance of

the couple over his shoulder. "Can you imagine if Em brought *him* home to her dad?"

Emily laughed, imaging the scene. "With my luck, my dad would let him move in. That guy looks like exactly like the type of person who would be building the World's Largest Collection of Bongs."

After the man walked in, the woman with him followed. Emily couldn't help but stare as she stepped into the diner.

The woman was lean and tall, almost two heads taller than the man she'd come in with. Her hair was short and spiky, sticking out all over her head and dyed a blue-black that seemed to shine under the neon lights of the restaurant. She was dressed like she'd just stepped out of one of the Matrix movies, with black leather pants, a long black trench coat, and heeled boots. Big red sunglasses covered her eyes, and the color on her lips was the same vibrant shade.

"Holy moly," Ana said, shaking her head. "Is there a costume party?"

Emily sighed. "I want to think so, I really do, but I don't."

At that moment, the waitress appeared with three towering parfait glasses expertly balanced on a tray. She set each down, then handed out spoons, straws, and a fresh pile of napkins. "There you go, hons. You kids enjoy. I'll be right back with your to-go cup and your check." She winked at Ana, who groaned and fell over onto Emily's shoulder.

"I can't even *look* at that, I'm so full," Ana whined.

"Oh, enough. Belly up to the bar, young lady." Emily

laughed and picked up both her straw and her spoon, then glanced at Brandon. "How do we even go about this?" she asked him.

Brandon shrugged and a big grin spread across his face. "I'm going in head first," he said.

Emily squealed as he did just that, plunging tongue into the top of the shake, licking out a giant scoop of whipped cream and chomping down on the two strawberries that garnished the top. She pulled her glass toward her and did the same, her nose suddenly covered in the sticky, sweet cream, her mouth flooded with strawberry.

Ana started pushing her out of the booth. "Gross!" She giggled. "You two are whipped cream *piglets!*"

Suddenly Emily was gasping and snorting whipped cream up her nose. "Wait!" she said, trying to catch her breath from laughing. "I'm about to asphyxiate on whipped cream!"

"Serves you right, you little oinker! Out of my booth. You have to go over there and sit with Brandon."

Emily laughed, obediently swinging around the end of the table while Brandon slid over to make room for her on his side. Ana pulled out her phone and began snapping pictures of the two of them while grunting like a pig between laughs.

If Emily had chosen a different method to start eating her dessert, one that didn't involve getting whipped cream all over her face, then maybe Ana wouldn't have felt compelled to send her to the other side of the table to sit with Brandon. Then she wouldn't have had her back to the door, and she might've been able to see what was going on before it hap-pened. She might've been able to stop it.

If Emily had just continued driving, and if they had gone past Rick's Diner and just stopped at a rest stop or some other fast-food restaurant for something to eat, then they wouldn't have been in the diner at all. If they weren't in the diner, they never would have gotten into the situation.

But it was all moot anyway, because she had turned off the highway, and they had decided to eat at that diner, and she had smashed her face into the whipped cream, and she had been sent to the other side of the table, where she couldn't see the front door.

And because she couldn't see the front door, she didn't see it when the woman with the spiky hair and long trench and the man with the chopped-up hoodie and excessive tat-toos pulled ski masks over their faces, raised two guns above their heads, and screamed over the noise of the restaurant:

"PUT YOUR HANDS IN THE AIR! THIS IS A ROBBERY!"

This definitely was *not* part of Emily's itinerary.

chapter 7

Emily threw her hands into the air, as did Brandon, but Ana just froze, her mouth hanging open. Emily felt her eyes go wide as she stared at Ana and hissed, "Hands. Up!"

But Ana looked at her as if a fuse had blown in her brain. "Wait. What? Who are those people?" she asked.

"They're . . . *bandits*." Even as the word escaped her lips in a whisper Emily felt Brandon turn to stare at her.

"Bandits?" he asked.

"Yes," she said under her breath. "Bandits."

"Not to split hairs, but don't bandits ride horses?" Brandon's eyes narrowed quizzically.

"Who *cares*?" Emily hissed. She looked at Ana. "Just put your hands up, like they said!"

The male bandit smashed his gun against the counter and yelled, "Open this register!"

As Emily and Brandon turned to see what was happening, Emily heard Ana give a short staccato shriek, and she realized that they had reached the point of no return when it came to Ana in any crisis, whether it was being present during an armed robbery or seeing a 40-percent-off sale at her favorite store in the mall. First was the confusion and disbelief, then the silence, and then . . . the shrieking.

This time Ana seemed to be attempting to control this by holding a hand over her mouth, which was actually helping to muffle the sound enough that it wasn't too obvious over the music coming from the jukebox in the corner. What *was* obvious was her other hand, which she had finally raised into the air, but was now waving it back and forth as if the bandits had asked a question and she just couldn't wait to be called on to give the answer.

"Ana!" Emily said in a low voice. "Stop. Waving. At. Them."

Emily turned back and saw one of the waitresses pulling all of the money out of the register . . . slowly. Too slowly for the woman in the long leather trench coat, it seemed, who waved her gun in the air and screamed, "Hurry it up!"

Tattoo Guy yelled, "Nobody move!" and Emily saw Trench Coat Lady begin to do wide sweeps of the restaurant with her gun pointed out in front of her. As the crazy-eyed lady with the spiky hair swung the pistol through the air and took a step forward, Emily flinched. It suddenly crossed her mind that she had never been in the same room as a gun—let alone witnessed a robbery, live and in progress. She could hear her heart pounding in her ears, and things seemed to slow down all around her, sort of like bobbing under water for a few moments and everything is muted and muffled.

As the waitress dumped wads of bills into the bag Tattoo Guy was holding, Trench Coat Lady was getting closer and closer to their table. Emily looked at Ana, who had now frozen, both hands over her head, and didn't appear to be breathing.

Emily could smell the leather coat as it brushed by their booth and she held her breath, waiting for the moment to be over, but the woman paused right next to their table, her mouth set into a thin line.

Emily bit down on her tongue and continued to hold her breath, trying to figure out what they'd done to grab the woman's attention, and what they could do to make sure they didn't keep it. Then, just as Trench Coat Lady was turning to walk away, Ana's phone sprang to life—loud, obnoxious, jump-out-of-our-skin life.

Never before had Emily felt so much hate toward Ana's insistence on having the most current pop songs as a ringtone on her phone. And Trench Coat Lady apparently felt the same way. She whirled back to the table and brought the butt of her pistol down on Ana's iPhone like a sledgehammer, sending tiny splinters of glass ricocheting in all directions across the table.

For a moment, the entire restaurant froze.

Emily felt like she was underwater again, floating in an endless second that suddenly snapped back to life with a piercing shriek from Ana, who grabbed the woman's wrist and screamed, "You BITCH!" Faster than Emily had ever seen anyone move, Ana pulled the gun out of Trench Coat Lady's hand and slid it across the table toward Emily, who caught it as she watched Ana's body sail from the booth and tackle the woman with the pointy black hair.

Just for a second Emily felt like she was watching a television show about a plucky teenage Latina vigilante who'd just decided to take matters into her own hands. This moment was interrupted when Brandon leaped onto the table, sending glasses of Strawberry Tsunami crashing in all directions. He jumped from the table to tackle Tattoo Guy, who had been just a yard to two away from reaching the spot where Ana and Trench Coat Lady were wrestling on the floor.

Almost without realizing what she was doing, as Ana and Trench Coat Lady screeched at each other and Brandon tried to pull the gun from Tattoo Guy's fist, Emily found herself standing on the seat of the booth, which was now covered in Strawberry Tsunami. When she realized that she was standing on the seat, a few other things also became clear to her:

1. She was holding a handgun.

2. She and her friends could very well die if she didn't do something *right now*.

3. If they were all dead, there would be no way to get to the party.

With barely any hesitation Emily jumped off the booth seat, landed next to where Tattoo Guy and Brandon were grunting on the floor, and swiftly kicked the gun from Tattoo Guy's hand, sending it sliding across the floor as Tattoo Guy let out a screech of pain. She was on her way to grab the gun from the floor when the loud, explosive crack of a gunshot sounded in the air.

Emily whirled around, a gun in each hand, and watched

as plaster rained down from the ceiling at the far end of the restaurant. There, standing by the door that led to the kitchen, was a gigantic man who had two hams for forearms and another for a neck. He was bald as a cue ball, with thick eyebrows and a goatee, and Emily was fairly certain even without asking that he owned a Harley Davidson. He was wearing a white apron smeared with food and holding a double-barreled shotgun, which he leveled in her direction.

"Get your hooligan friends and get the hell out of my diner!"

Emily blinked hard and opened her mouth to protest, when she followed the man's eyes to her own hands and saw a gun in each one. It was time for the next horrible realization:

4. He thought *she* was the bandit.

Had she not been holding a pistol in each hand, Emily might have tried to explain. She might have protested, or smiled and assured the man with the shotgun that this was all a misunderstanding—a giant miscommunication. Instead she dropped both guns on the floor, turned to the door, and ran.

chapter 8

Emily exited the diner only three steps ahead of Brandon. Tattoo Guy had reached down to scoop up both of the guns Emily had dropped, and behind him Ana and Trench Coat Lady tumbled out the door in a tangle of arms and legs. Ana was screaming and trying to pull the ski mask off of the woman who, Emily realized, had a fist full of Ana's long black hair. Tattoo Guy was yelling through his ski mask and trying to pull Trench Coat Lady off Ana. Brandon was shouting at Ana to get in the freaking car, and Ana, who really might have gone insane at that moment, was still screaming about her broken iPhone.

Then there was the other sound Emily heard that rose over the fracas happening in front of her. With her heart pounding faster than ever, she held up her hands and screamed, "Everybody shut the hell up!"

Amazingly, even Ana and Trench Coat Lady stopped trying to claw each other, and they all turned and looked at Emily, breathing hard. Emily cocked her head and raised her eyebrows, watching as the recognition flooded each of their faces when the newfound silence allowed them to hear the growing wail of sirens.

"Shit," Brandon and Tattoo Guy said at the same time, breaking the group's silence.

There was another moment's pause, and then they were all racing through the parking lot.

Emily reached the car and slid behind the steering wheel, then popped the locks and heard the doors open and close as she slammed her key into the ignition and started the car. As the doors slammed shut, she pressed her foot down on the gas pedal and pulled out of the parking lot at top speed. It was only then that she glanced in the rearview mirror and was shocked to see that it wasn't Brandon looking back at her.

"What the hell are they doing in my car?" Emily screamed, her eyes locked on the two bandits in her backseat. She was starting to pull over when Brandon yelled back.

"Keep going!" he shouted. "Do not stop!"

"I want these assholes out of my car," Emily said. "Why did you even let them in here?"

"Um . . . guns?"

"We are going straight to an Apple store so this bitch can buy me a new iPhone," Ana said from the passenger seat. She turned and shouted into the back, "You hear me? You're getting me a new phone!"

"You are gonna have to let that go," Brandon said.

Emily spun the car around and was back on the highway in a second, figuring that should make it much more difficult for anyone to follow them, now that they were lost among the other cars speeding down the road.

"Fast thinking back there," Tattoo Guy said as he patted her should.

"Yeah," Trench Coat Lady chimed in. "You can drive my getaway car anytime."

"Oh my God." Emily couldn't believe her ears. "Is this really happening? All I wanted to do was get to this party, and now I'm *harboring criminals*."

"Who . . . us?" Tattoo Guy pulled off his ski mask.

"No," Emily said. "The serial killers in the trunk. YES, you!"

"Oh please." Trench Coat Lady pulled of her ski mask too. "We're not criminals. And you don't have to harbor us, just drop us off at the next exit." The woman had a deep red scratch across her cheek, and Emily was glad that Ana had managed to inflict at least a little bit of pain.

"What do you mean you're not criminals?" Ana said. "I'm pretty sure what you did to my phone counts as a serious crime!"

"Not to mention the armed robbery," Brandon said.

"Look!" Tattoo Guy popped open the chamber of each of his guns. "We don't even have bullets in here." He handed both over to Brandon.

"Huh," Brandon said. "He's right. These are empty."

"No police officer in the *world* cares whether those weapons were loaded or not," Emily said. "You were still robbing the place."

Trench Coat Lady sighed. "The point is that we weren't planning to *hurt* anyone."

"Yeah," said Tattoo Guy. "I'm real sorry about all this. It's kind of all a misunderstanding, right? Anyway, my name's Chestnut. This here's Liz."

Emily glanced in the rearview mirror and saw Liz give a small wave. "We're really sorry we got started off on the wrong foot."

"The wrong foot?" Emily was trying not to yell, but her heart was still racing and she was certain that a highway patrolman was going to come speeding up behind her at any moment, even after her apparently top-notch getaway tactics. "Calling someone the wrong name, or spilling a beverage on them as you shake hands is the 'wrong foot.' Holding us at gunpoint is not the *wrong foot*. It's a *felony*."

"I understand how you feel," Chestnut said solemnly.

"No. No, I don't think you do," said Ana. "My iPhone is dead." She waved the shattered screen in his direction. "It won't even turn on!"

"At least you thought to pick it up," Brandon said. "Thank God the cops don't have your phone."

"Even so," Emily said. "Exactly how long do you think it will take before the police go over the security footage from the cameras that place must have had and run my license plate? Or just plaster our faces all over the news. I'm not even out of high school yet and I'm going to be tried as an adult for aiding and abetting!"

"Nah," snorted Chestnut, shaking his head. "Besides, Liz and I ain't horrible folks. We're high school sweethearts, ya know. Good people."

"No, I didn't know," said Emily. "And somehow, I think that under cross-examination, that little tidbit will be ruled irrelevant."

"High school sweethearts? *Aw . . .*"

Emily glanced at Ana, who was now on her knees in the front seat with her chin on the headrest, staring at Liz with what could only be described as googly eyes.

"It's true," brayed Liz. "He asked me to prom fifteen years ago and the rest is history."

"Did you start robbing banks and restaurants right after the dance, or did you have special training in college first?" Emily couldn't help herself. Now that she knew there was no ammo in the guns, they didn't seem nearly as dangerous, and she decided to take a few shots of her own.

"Now see? Right there. You've got us all wrong, little missy." Chestnut turned to Brandon. "She always like this?"

"Snippy?" Brandon asked him. "Yeah, pretty much."

"Oh my God, Brandon. Whose side are you on?"

"We have never robbed a bank," said Liz. "And never would."

"Like to keep our hits smaller than that," Chestnut explained. "Don't wanna get caught being too greedy. Like to hit little spots where there's less money and less security, too. Just to make a nice life."

"You're like Bonnie and Clyde," squealed Ana.

"It *is* sorta romantic, Em," Brandon said sheepishly.

Emily rolled her eyes, "It is not. There's nothing romantic about this. And don't call me 'Em.'"

"Look," said Chestnut, "all we want is to have a little fun, make a little dough, and take care of our boy."

"Your boy?" Emily asked. "Oh my God, you're *parents*?" She was horrified.

"Oh, don't act so high and mighty," said Liz. "We love Artie just as much as your parents love you."

"How old is he?" asked Brandon.

"Five," said Chestnut.

"Wanna see a picture?"

Before Emily knew what was happening, Liz was passing her phone around the car, showing off pictures of Artie. Ana and Brandon were saying how cute he was and Emily realized she was alone in her understanding of just how far off the rails this day had actually gone. There was one thing and one thing only that she wanted at this point: these nut jobs out of the car.

"Okay, everyone. I hate to interrupt the offspring love fest, but, Liz? Chestnut? Where are you getting out, because I want to get you there fast."

"Well, our next stop was gonna be the Little-J Mart at the next exit up," Chestnut said with a shrug. "Don't s'pose you could drop us off there, could you?"

"Sure we could," Brandon said.

Before she could protest, Ana had held up a hand at Brandon. "Uh-uh," she said. "Not so fast, Speedy Gonzales." She turned to Liz and smiled sweetly. "Miss O'Brien's Criminal Cab Service will be happy to deliver you to your next hold-up location, but it'll cost you."

Chestnut squinted across the back seat at Ana. "How much," he asked.

"The amount of one new iPhone," Ana said smugly.

Liz looked at Chestnut, who stared back at her and then shrugged. Liz reached into the bag the waitress had filled with cash from the register and counted out a fistful of twenties to Ana, who smiled like she'd won an Olympic medal.

"Pleasure doing business with you," Ana said, then turned to Emily. "Tell the chick behind the steering wheel where we're going."

chapter 9

Emily couldn't believe she was letting herself be talked into this. All she wanted was to be back on the road headed toward the party. "Where the hell is this Little-J Mart?"

"Also, *what* the hell is a Little-J Mart?" Ana asked.

"Is it like a K-Mart's kid brother?"

"Brandon! This is not funny." He clearly wasn't taking this seriously enough.

"Actually . . . ," he said.

Ana glanced back at Brandon in the backseat and started giggling. Chestnut and Liz joined in.

"I mean, what's the big deal, Emily?" Brandon said. "We're gonna take them to their next stop and drop them off."

"'Course, if ya'll wanna help us out a little by distracting the cashier," suggested Chestnut, "we'd be much obliged."

"Why not?" Brandon said casually, shrugging.

Emily felt like she was about to lose control of the car. Not literally—her hands were both still in the ten and two position on the steering wheel—but internally, she felt as though they were tumbling end over end down the embankment in the middle of the highway. "Why not?" she yelled, shaking her head. "There are so many reasons why not I can't even list them. There isn't enough time in the rest of my life to tell you all the reasons why *not!*"

"Oh c'mon," said Brandon, borderline whining. "They don't even have any bullets. It's not like *we're* gonna rob the place. Nobody's gonna get hurt. Besides, what a freaking incredible story to tell when we get to college."

"*If* we get to college," said Emily. "We'll be lucky not to spend the rest of our teens and twenties behind bars."

In the distance Emily saw a big sign looming over the next exit ramp, a lowercase *j* lit from within. Chestnut pointed and said, "That's it up there."

"So, quick question," Ana said. She seemed much more calm, now that she had payment for her phone. "How do you guys normally get around? Why didn't you get into your own car?"

"We didn't have one," Liz said. "Normally we use cabs. They're great. You grab the cash and run outside, then just hide for a bit. People assume that you sped away in your getaway car, when really we just call up a taxi and they take us out of there, no problem."

"And the drivers don't mind being an accessory to grand larceny?" Emily asked

"Grand what?"

Emily sighed as Chestnut piped up. "Aw hell. There's nothing grand about any of our robbing folks. Don't usually get away with more than a few thousand bucks—and that's if we're lucky."

"So what's your plan?" Brandon asked.

"Plan?" Chestnut shrugged. "We'll see what we can get from the mart, then get a cab after. Same as always."

They were pulling up to the Little-J Mart, and Emily was about to pull into the parking lot, but Brandon stopped her and directed her to drive past the convenience store and closer to a small metal building next door, finally telling her to shut off the car there.

"What are we doing?" Emily asked, though she wasn't sure she wanted to know. "We could've just dropped them off."

"Don't want cameras catching a glimpse of the license plate, right?" Brandon said.

Emily nodded, sort of impressed. At least he was thinking now.

"Okay, Liz and Chestnut, it was great meeting you, we had so much fun, please keep in touch, say hello to Artie for us, you can get out of the car now." Emily put on the biggest grin possible as she turned around and looked at them in the backseat. "Don't forget to keep your ski masks firmly in place."

"Wait, wait," Brandon said. "We're going too."

"Excuse me?" Emily wasn't sure she'd heard right. "Didn't we *just* conclude that we're not getting involved."

"We won't really be involved," Brandon said. He looked at Liz and Chestnut like they were his new closest friends. "So here's the deal. We'll go into the shop and do some looking around, case the place, whatever, you know? And then you guys will follow. We'll cause a sufficient enough commotion in there so you can get your money and get out, and then we'll follow afterward, after calming down the clerk and things like that. In and out. Easy."

"Sounds like a plan to me," Chestnut said.

"It sounds *dangerous*," Emily said loudly.

"Come on, Em," said Brandon. "YOLO, right?"

"No." Emily shook her head. "Not at all."

Ana grabbed Emily's shoulder and pleaded. "Come on. It might be kind of fun. And it's not like we're *doing* anything. No one will get hurt, and right afterward we can be on our way to the party again."

Emily looked at the clock and shook her head. They were already off schedule time-wise. And she had the feeling Brandon and Ana weren't going to let up, and the faster she could get Chestnut and Liz out of her car, the better. They could do the plan just as Brandon said, and then as Chestnut and Liz went off in their taxi, Emily, Ana, and Brandon could get back on the highway and head straight for the Steins', with no stops along the way.

"Okay, fine," she said. "Let's just get this over with."

They all piled out of the car together, then quickly made their way toward the mart. Ana was bouncing with excitement, and Brandon seemed pretty pumped too. Emily was excited, but only because this was marking the end of a very horrible, very time-consuming sidetrack in their one-day road trip.

At the door Brandon entered first, and then Ana. Emily

stood outside for a moment, taking a few deep breaths and trying to convince herself that she wasn't ruining her life, and that she wasn't stepping into a trap, and that she wasn't going to get arrested in the next five minutes. Nothing she could say to herself really convinced her of any of these things, but eventually she just had to suck it up and take the step, walking into the chilled air of the small convenience store.

In one corner she saw Brandon with an armful of candy bars, Corn Nuts, and Doritos in different flavors. She scanned the store for Ana and then saw her at the counter under the register on her hands and knees, her face being licked by a Chihuahua whose entire body seemed to be wagging.

Emily made a beeline for Brandon, who handed her a handful of smoked almonds and an assortment of Skittles and M&Ms in different varieties. "Are you *high*?" she asked him. "We just ate a kabillion calories."

Brandon shrugged. "Excitement makes me hungry."

"This is nothing to be excited about."

"Sure it is! We're about to witness a holdup with no bullets." Brandon moved on to the Slim Jim section of the snack aisle.

Emily turned around just in time to see Ana jump up and shriek as the Chihuahua began to dribble pee all over the floor in excitement. Emily wasn't the only one to observe this. A wiry man with a trucker's hat and a pronounced overbite appeared from behind the counter and growled with rage. "PICKLES!" A pointy cowboy boot shot out and caught Pickles in the ribs. He yelped in pain and raced to hide behind Ana's legs.

chapter 10

"Open the door! Open the door!" Ana was jumping up and down and screaming at the top of her lungs.

"I can't." Emily stood there, staring at the driver's side door, watching Ana's head bounce up and down. She might have burst into tears except that Ana was still jumping up and down, Pickles clutched to her breasts, both her head and the dog's popping over the roof of the car into sight for a brief moment and then disappearing completely. Every time she jumped, Pickles let out a little yelp. The effect was just comical enough to keep her from breaking down completely.

The crinkling of snack bags and pounding of feet came seconds later as Brandon sprinted toward the car, his arms filled with a couple bags of Doritos and a bottle of Coke. Before Emily could say anything about being unable to get into the car, the beep of the doors unlocking sounded, and she grinned when she saw the glint of the keys in Brandon's hand.

Emily and Ana both pulled their doors open, and Brandon shoved Emily over into the passenger seat on top of Ana as he slid into the driver's seat and shoved the keys into the ignition.

"What are you doing?" Emily yelled as her lap was suddenly

"Hey!" Ana yelled. Her eyes were flashing fire as she reached down and scooped up the tiny dog in her arms. Emily wanted to stop all this somehow, to push the rewind/erase button on the past hour of their day, but there wasn't anything she could do.

"Damn dog!" The man with the buckteeth and the cowboy boots was wiping up Pickles's piddle with paper towels. As Emily approached, she noticed his nametag read EARL and wondered what the best way would be to get them all out of the store before Chestnut and Liz barged in. While she tried to come up with a plan, Ana begin to harangue Earl about kicking a canine.

"He didn't do anything to you," she said.

"Pissed on my clean floor," Earl shot back. "I hate that damn dog. Girlfriend left him when she ran off with my mechanic."

"I'd leave your sorry ass too," Ana said, kissing the top of Pickles's head.

"Maybe Pickles needs to go outside to finish his business." Emily tried to sound helpful, and Ana turned toward the door as if this was a good idea. Emily dropped the armful of snacks Brandon had given her onto the counter. "Hey, Brandon! Let's get going!" she called toward him. He was holding three bottles of Coke in place with his chin on top of the giant pile of junk food in his arms, and he was walking her way. Emily began to wonder if she had gained a foothold on the sheer rock wall of this impossible situation, but as she turned back to help Ana out the door with Pickles, she saw two familiar ski masks burst through the entrance.

"HANDS UP, ASSHOLES! THIS IS A ROBBERY!"

Brandon was as unprepared for this as Emily was, and he jumped about six inches into the air. The entire front of the store was showered with Doritos and Slim Jims and sodas. One of the bottles hit Earl in the back of the neck as he leaped up from cleaning the floor, and he knocked his head on the underside of the counter. He fell back to his knees, unleashing a stream of curses.

"Get up!" Liz shouted at him, waiving her gun in his face.

"Open the register, numb nuts!" Chestnut started prodding Earl with the barrel of his pistol.

Emily stood in the doorway next to Ana, unsure what to do next. Brandon was staring at Liz and Chestnut, too, as if they were going to give him a step-by-step on how to successfully rob a convenience store without ammunition.

As it turns out, the only person who was sure exactly what to do next was Earl. He was still swearing and rubbing his head with one hand, but he scrambled behind the counter, reached underneath, and pulled out a gun of his own. Of course, Earl's gun *did* have bullets in it, which he proved in short order by beginning to fire wildly in all directions.

Emily threw both hands into the air for the second time that day and screamed. As she did, her keys flew out of her hands and landed in the rubble of Brandon's junk food mountain. Without pausing, she turned, pushed Ana through the

doors, and raced past the convenience store gas pumps. heard the sound of Ana behind her, but it wasn't until she run into the alley next door and was in sight of her car she fully comprehended the problem at hand: Her keys w still in the Little-J, lost somewhere on the floor under a pil Frito-Lay products.

"Hey!" Ana yelled. Her eyes were flashing fire as she reached down and scooped up the tiny dog in her arms. Emily wanted to stop all this somehow, to push the rewind/erase button on the past hour of their day, but there wasn't anything she could do.

"Damn dog!" The man with the buckteeth and the cowboy boots was wiping up Pickles's piddle with paper towels. As Emily approached, she noticed his nametag read EARL and wondered what the best way would be to get them all out of the store before Chestnut and Liz barged in. While she tried to come up with a plan, Ana begin to harangue Earl about kicking a canine.

"He didn't do anything to you," she said.

"Pissed on my clean floor," Earl shot back. "I hate that damn dog. Girlfriend left him when she ran off with my mechanic."

"I'd leave your sorry ass too," Ana said, kissing the top of Pickles's head.

"Maybe Pickles needs to go outside to finish his business." Emily tried to sound helpful, and Ana turned toward the door as if this was a good idea. Emily dropped the armful of snacks Brandon had given her onto the counter. "Hey, Brandon! Let's get going!" she called toward him. He was holding three bottles of Coke in place with his chin on top of the giant pile of junk food in his arms, and he was walking her way. Emily began to wonder if she had gained a foothold on the sheer rock wall of this impossible situation, but as she turned back to help Ana out the door with Pickles, she saw two familiar ski masks burst through the entrance.

"HANDS UP, ASSHOLES! THIS IS A ROBBERY!"

Brandon was as unprepared for this as Emily was, and he jumped about six inches into the air. The entire front of the store was showered with Doritos and Slim Jims and sodas. One of the bottles hit Earl in the back of the neck as he leaped up from cleaning the floor, and he knocked his head on the underside of the counter. He fell back to his knees, unleashing a stream of curses.

"Get up!" Liz shouted at him, waiving her gun in his face.

"Open the register, numb nuts!" Chestnut started prodding Earl with the barrel of his pistol.

Emily stood in the doorway next to Ana, unsure what to do next. Brandon was staring at Liz and Chestnut, too, as if they were going to give him a step-by-step on how to successfully rob a convenience store without ammunition.

As it turns out, the only person who was sure exactly what to do next was Earl. He was still swearing and rubbing his head with one hand, but he scrambled behind the counter, reached underneath, and pulled out a gun of his own. Of course, Earl's gun *did* have bullets in it, which he proved in short order by beginning to fire wildly in all directions.

Emily threw both hands into the air for the second time that day and screamed. As she did, her keys flew out of her hands and landed in the rubble of Brandon's junk food mountain. Without pausing, she turned, pushed Ana through the doors, and raced past the convenience store gas pumps. She heard the sound of Ana behind her, but it wasn't until she had run into the alley next door and was in sight of her car that she fully comprehended the problem at hand: Her keys were still in the Little-J, lost somewhere on the floor under a pile of Frito-Lay products.

chapter 10

"Open the door! Open the door!" Ana was jumping up and down and screaming at the top of her lungs.

"I can't." Emily stood there, staring at the driver's side door, watching Ana's head bounce up and down. She might have burst into tears except that Ana was still jumping up and down, Pickles clutched to her breasts, both her head and the dog's popping over the roof of the car into sight for a brief moment and then disappearing completely. Every time she jumped, Pickles let out a little yelp. The effect was just comical enough to keep her from breaking down completely.

The crinkling of snack bags and pounding of feet came seconds later as Brandon sprinted toward the car, his arms filled with a couple bags of Doritos and a bottle of Coke. Before Emily could say anything about being unable to get into the car, the beep of the doors unlocking sounded, and she grinned when she saw the glint of the keys in Brandon's hand.

Emily and Ana both pulled their doors open, and Brandon shoved Emily over into the passenger seat on top of Ana as he slid into the driver's seat and shoved the keys into the ignition.

"What are you doing?" Emily yelled as her lap was suddenly

full of convenience-store snacks, dumped there by Brandon, and a Chihuahua from Ana's arms.

"Driving!" Brandon yelled. Just as he threw the car in gear, the back door opened and Chestnut and Liz tumbled into the backseat, whooping as Brandon peeled out into the alley and shot through a yellow light across the service road and onto the on-ramp.

"Are you trying to *kill us*?" Ana screeched almost as loudly as the tires had.

"Kill you?" Brandon asked. "I'm trying to save your ass. In case you didn't notice, that asshole was shooting real bullets at us."

"But he missed!" Liz was giggling like a hyena, and Chestnut was still whooping like a drunk frat boy.

Emily stared at them in her backseat and felt a certainty that she was cursed. How else could it be this difficult to get rid of these crackpots? It was like she was a magnet for crazy today, the one day when all she really wanted was to stick to the schedule.

Emily saw a sign that said REST STOP: 1 MILE. She pointed at it and said, "We're stopping there."

"No way!" Brandon said. "That dude called the police for sure."

"Yeah!" said Chestnut, suddenly serious. "We can't stop anywhere around here."

Emily started punching Brandon in the shoulder.

"Ow!" he yelped, the car swerving wildly. "Stop!"

"YOU STOP!" Emily snapped. She kept punching his shoulder. Ana shrieked. Pickles barked.

"You're going to make him run off the road!" Liz reached over the seat and tried to stop Emily from punching Brandon by grabbing her arm.

"Keep your hands off me!" shrieked Emily, turning around and slapping wildly into the air. She didn't care where her hands fell. She wanted these nitwits out of the car and she wanted to be on her way to the party. Period. If that meant she had to throw a fit to make it happen, so be it.

The lights of the rest area were coming up on their right as Chestnut grabbed at Emily's wrists, trying to hold them to keep from getting slapped.

"BRANDON!" Ana shrieked. "PULL OVER!"

"NO!" Liz and Chestnut yelled in unison.

Emily turned around and slid an arm around Brandon's neck, pulling his head towards her until she could whisper in his ear. "So help me God, Brandon Kinney, if you don't pull off at this rest stop I will open the door and jump out onto the shoulder and take Ana with me." To be honest, the tone in her own voice scared Emily. On some level she realized she was serious—and how weird it was to be pushed to a place where she would risk her own safety to change what was happening.

"Fine," Brandon said with a deep breath. He'd heard an eerie quality in Emily's threat that he'd never heard before, and it scared him. He put on the blinker and eased the car down the exit ramp into the rest-stop parking lot.

The parking lot was mainly deserted except for a couple of semis parked down at the end, past the blond-brick service building. Brandon pulled into a space right in front of a well-lit area with five vending machines and signs pointing in opposite directions towards the men's and women's bathrooms.

"Asshole!" Chestnut punched the back of the seat.

"HEY!" Ana whirled, shoving Emily into the dashboard and Pickles onto Brandon's lap. "He just drove your getaway car!"

"Some getaway," said Liz. "We didn't even get any cash before that numb nuts back there started shooting."

"And whose fault is *that*?" Ana asked. "Not Brandon's."

Liz and Chestnut both hung their heads sheepishly under Ana's glare. Chestnut reached for the door handle. Liz grabbed his arm. "Where are you going?"

"Aw hell," said Chestnut. "I need a smoke."

Chestnut threw open the car door and went stomping up to a picnic table near the snack machines, where he pulled out a pack of cigarettes and a lighter. Liz went scrambling after him.

"Well, that was a total bust," said Brandon.

"You think?" Emily said. She rolled her eyes and sighed the word "Idiots" under her breath.

"Hey! Who're you calling 'idiots'?" Brandon said, pulling open a family-size bag of Cool Ranch Doritos.

Emily couldn't stand it anymore. "You! Them! Everyone." She reached over Ana and pulled the door handle open. "Jesus Christ, Ana, get out of the car. I am crushed against this console."

"Alright, alright. *Cálmate.*" Ana slid out of the car, and Emily practically tumbled onto the pavement after her.

"Don't you tell *me* to calm down, Ana. I just wanted us to have a good time at a party this weekend, which, might I remind you *both*, I am paying for gas to drive us to."

Brandon walked around the front of the car and leaned against the hood, holding the bag of Doritos out to Emily. "Chips?"

Emily wheeled on him. "How can you eat *all the time?*"

Brandon shrugged and took a glug from a two-liter bottle of Coke. He let out a giant burp that smelled like rotten Cool Ranch, then made that goofy grin. Ana immediately collapsed into giggles and Emily punched Brandon in the arm.

"Ow! Hey, you have to stop that. Why can girls beat up on guys all the time, when we're not allowed to hit back?"

"Oh, I don't know, Brandon," Emily scoffed. "Maybe it's because doofus guys do idiotic things like *offering to take the robbers who hold up the diner to their next hit!*"

"Good job, Pickles! That's a good poo poo!" Ana was squealing as Pickles did his business, then started running across the grassy lawn.

"Where are you going?" Emily asked.

Ana stopped and pointed to a big green bin with a picture of a dog on it by the trash cans. "To get a poop bag over there."

"Oh," Emily said, "so it's okay to collude with bandits and become an accomplice to armed robbery, but *picking up dog poop* is where you *draw the line?*"

"Fine," Ana huffed. "I'll leave the dog poop."

"Oh, that's not all we're leaving," Emily said, g
keys from Brandon.

"We're leaving?" Emily heard Chestnut's voice, and whirled around to see him and Liz walking up to the car, smelling like an ashtray.

"No," said Emily. "*You're* not leaving. *We* are leaving. *You* are going to continue your life of crime using someone else for transportation."

"You can't leave us *here!*" Liz said, alarmed.

"Oh yes. Yes, we can."

"But we have one more job today!" Liz was frantic.

Emily stalked up to Liz and leaned into her face. "If you get into the backseat of my car ever again, I swear to God I will call the police on you myself and wait until they show up to slap you in cuffs."

"But what about our little boy?" Chestnut said. "They'll take Artie away from us."

Emily glared at him. "Well, if you can't stop stealing from people, maybe they *should* take Artie away from you." Emily walked around the front of the car, got in behind the driver's seat, and started the engine.

Brandon offered Chestnut the bag of Doritos. "Hang on a sec," he said. "I'll talk to her."

Chestnut took it and dug in with Liz while Brandon leaned down and rapped on the passenger-side window with a knuckle.

Emily rolled down the window a few inches. "Get. In. *Now*." She was not screwing around.

"I'd really like to," Brandon said like he was breaking bad news to a child. "It's just that I can't leave them here by themselves."

"You have *got* to be *kidding me*." Emily laid her head on the steering wheel. The clock told her that her plan was already almost two hours off schedule, and if everything that had just happened hadn't convinced her, for some reason seeing the time made her understand just what an unmitigated disaster this day had become.

Ana pulled open the passenger door and jumped in with Pickles, who did a very happy wiggle dance into Emily's lap and licked her on the nose. It was such a ridiculous thing—that a dog was dancing around her front seat and licking her face—that she gave up. She just started laughing. Ana watched her for a second, her eyes wide. Emily was sure that Ana must think that she was watching her best friend lose her mind, but then Ana was laughing too—and neither one of them could stop. Eventually, there were tears running down Emily's face, and Ana kept panting, "Stop! Okay, stop! My stomach hurts from—" Then Pickles jumped up and licked her nose with a little bark and the two of them collapsed into hysterics again.

Finally Brandon opened the door to the backseat and slid inside. "Are we good to go?" he asked. "Can I tell them to get in?"

"Dammit, Brandon. Why do you care about these assholes more than your friends' safety?" Emily said. She wasn't angry now, she was just curious. It didn't make sense to her.

Brandon shrugged. "I dunno," he said. "I just know that when my dad left, my mom . . ." His voice trailed off for a second, and Emily saw a shadow cross his face. She saw Ana reach into the backseat and put her hand on Brandon's knee. Feeling her touch him, he looked up into her eyes, and somehow found his voice again. "My mom, she was strapped financially. I know she did some stuff that she wasn't proud of. I mean, she didn't sell herself or anything, but she worked a lot of shifts at the Bikini Bar. I just understand when people feel like they don't have any options left to take care of their kid."

Part of her wanted to protest, but Emily kept her mouth closed. True, they didn't even know if Artie existed, and there were obvious problems with equating Liz and Chestnut with Brandon's mom, who had worked her ass off to keep things going for Brandon and not lose their house after his dad ran off . . . but still, she was tired of the arguments—with her friends, sure, but mainly with herself.

Emily sighed. "Where do they want to go next?"

"Well . . ." Brandon had a sheepish grin on his face. "They have one more job planned."

"Brandon," Emily said, "they are *so bad* at holdups."

This cracked Ana up again, and this time when the laughter spread through the car, Brandon was in on it too. "*Dude.* I *know*," he said. Finally they settled down again, and when they did, they saw Chestnut and Liz leaning against the front of the car making out. Emily started to say "Ewww!" but stopped herself, and watched the tender way Chestnut held Liz, one arm around her waist, one hand sliding up to cup her cheek.

"Aww, they're so *cute!*" Ana said, squeezing Pickles, who yelped in agreement.

Something about this moment gave Emily pause. Sure, they were criminals, but maybe the things people *did* didn't define who they actually *were*. She thought about Brandon's mom slinging drinks at the Bikini Bar until she met Brandon's stepdad and could go back to school and finish her teaching degree. True, Brandon's mom hadn't done anything illegal, but she'd done whatever it took to make sure Brandon had everything he needed.

"They may be cute," Emily said, "but you guys, it's too dangerous to keep hanging out with them."

"Agreed," said Brandon. "Just let them tell you about this last job?"

Looking back, Emily would understand that this was the moment she stopped trying. Everybody was always telling her to "let go" and "go with the flow."

"Fine," she said.

Brandon opened the door and poked his head out. "Jesus, you two. Get a *room* why don't you."

Liz giggled, and Emily actually thought she might have seen her blush. She and Chestnut came barreling into the backseat.

"So, you're gonna take us to the last job?" Liz asked.

Emily sighed. "Where is this last stop?"

Chestnut jumped in, his eyes lit up like fireworks. "Well, see, we gotta get to this big warehouse about five miles up the highway. We've got to make a pickup."

"Whoa, whoa, whoa." Ana held up her hand. "Pick up *what?*"

Liz and Chestnut glanced at each other. "A shipment," said Liz brightly. She started tapping around on her phone. "Let me pull up the address."

"A shipment of *what* exactly?" asked Emily.

"Coke," said Chestnut.

"Don't you need a truck to pick up a bunch of soda?" asked Ana. Emily stared at her friend. *How could she be this naive?* Chestnut almost busted a gut, and Liz was snorting she was laughing so hard.

"Oh, sweetheart." Liz patted Ana's head. "*Cocaine.* Blow."

"Wow," Brandon whistled quietly. "You guys are like, big time, huh?"

Chestnut shrugged. "Not yet, but we're hoping to be."

"Do you guys run drugs a lot?" Ana asked. Emily couldn't help being concerned by the curiosity in her voice. *Is Ana really weighing the pros and cons of felony possession?*

"Well, this is our first time," said Liz. "But we hear these guys aren't the scary cartel types."

Emily glanced into the rearview mirror and saw Brandon's eyes go wide. "You mean, you've never met these dudes before?" Emily was pleased that he seemed a little bit scared. Maybe all those hours watching *Breaking Bad* had put the fear of God in him where the drug trade was concerned.

"We can take care of ourselves." Liz was all swagger and bluster.

Emily held up both hands. This conversation was going no further. "Okay, you guys. It's been great and all. I think it's pretty clear that we aren't being pursued, so that guy Earl at Little-J must not have gotten our license plate."

"Or maybe he didn't call the police," said Brandon.

"Either way, our little crime spree ends here." Emily's voice was firm. "I really just want to get to the party."

"Wait—what party?" Liz asked.

"Oh, it's no big deal." Emily sighed. She knew it was unattractive, but she couldn't help the sarcasm that oozed from her voice. "It's just going to be the best high-school party that has ever been thrown in the history of high-school parties."

"C'mon," groaned Brandon. "How do you even know that?"

"Look at how much trouble we've had getting to it," said Emily. "If we've gone through this much shit to even *show up*, don't you think it's going to *have* to be worth it? I mean, isn't that the universal law of parties?"

"Just take us to the next gas station." Everybody turned and looked at Liz.

"Aw hell, no, babe," Chestnut started to protest, but Liz raised a hand to his face, and Chestnut immediately shut up even though Liz was still staring at Emily. There was a faraway look in her eyes. Emily felt like Liz was almost staring right through her.

"I remember," Liz said to her.

"What?" Emily was confused.

"A party my senior year," said Liz. "That's where I met this one." She slid an arm around Chestnut and planted another kiss on his cheek. "Drop us at the Arco up at the next exit. We'll call a cab and have it take us back to our car."

"Wait," said Ana. "You have a car? Why did you say you take cabs?"

"Well, our car doesn't always *work* so well," Liz explained. "But it was working today. We parked down the street from Rick's. We can just have a cab take us back there."

"Are you sure?" Brandon asked. "I mean we could—"

"We're sure," said Liz. "You guys need to get going. You never know who might be at the best party of your high-school years."

Emily smiled at Liz. For the first time since this freaky chick with the spiky hair had blazed into the diner with an empty gun over her head and a ski mask over her face, Emily felt an understanding had passed between them.

"Well, step on it!" Liz commanded. "Can't keep destiny waiting."

chapter 11

As they drove away from Liz and Chestnut, Ana held Pickles up to the window and waived his tiny front paws at them.

"What are we going to do with that dog?" Emily asked.

Ana looked horrified. "We are going to take it home with us."

"Ana, your mom barely lets humans into her home, and we have to take off our shoes *and* our socks. There is no way in hell she's letting you keep a Chihuahua. Especially one named Pickles you found in a gas station."

"Yeah." Brandon laughed. "Em has a point."

"Don't call me that," said Emily.

"And don't *you* be such a spoilsport about my dog," Ana said.

"Ana, it's not even *your* dog," Emily said. "You *stole* it."

"All I know is that any man who would kick this beautiful boy should not be considered worthy of a second thought. Neither should any *puta* who would leave her dog with that scumbag." Ana nuzzled Pickles close to her chin while Brandon fed him a Dorito. "He's much better off with me."

Emily started to point out that there wasn't even any way to explain to Ana's mother where the dog came from without incriminating all of them, but Brandon's cell phone let out a shrill ring in the backseat.

"Brandon?" Emily said. "Are you going to get that?"

"Get what?"

"Your phone, *pendejo*," said Ana. "It's ringing."

"No, it's not." Brandon held up his phone. "It's one of yours."

"My phone is crushed into a kajillion pieces," Ana reminded him.

"Shit." Brandon held up a phone. "This must be Liz's. We have to go back. Maybe we can still catch them at the gas station."

"No way in hell." Emily sped up a little. She was finally on the highway and she was not going to stop again until the beautiful sight of the Steins' mountain mansion swung into full view.

"Are you sure?" asked Ana.

"If we take back that phone, we take back that dog." As she said the words, Emily knew they would knock Ana out of the argument. She could handle Brandon on her own.

"You play dirty," Ana said, her eyes narrowed.

"That's so cold," said Brandon.

"What? How is that *cold*?" Emily was so tired of feeling like the stick-in-the-mud. She was tired of being exasperated with her friends. She took a deep breath. "All I want is to get to this party, is that okay? We are already two hours behind schedule. If we're lucky, we'll have an hour when we get there to freshen up and pull our outfits together."

"Wait—outfits?" said Brandon. "You're not wearing that?"

Emily looked at Ana. "Do you want to take this one, or shall I?"

Ana shook her head. "Ay, *mamacita*. He's hopeless."

"Me?" yelped Brandon. "*I'm* hopeless? You two are talking about outfit changes and a party like it's so important. I just want to get this poor woman's phone back to her. I mean, for chrissakes, she's robbing gas stations to feed her *kid*. She doesn't have money for a new phone."

"I honestly can't tell if you're serious," said Emily. "Just in case you are, lemme break this down for you. First off, if we turn around now and go back, the chances are very slim that Liz will still be at the Arco."

"Well, we can just go back and meet them at the diner," Brandon said.

"Have you lost your mind?" shrieked Ana. "That place must be crawling with cops by now."

Brandon sighed. "I just don't feel right about it. I mean, she did pay you back for *your* phone."

"Yeah," said Ana. "Because she smashed it to *smithereens* with a *gun* which she was using to *hold up a diner*."

"I really think Liz will find another phone to use," said Emily.

"Can't we at least call Chestnut's phone from her phone and—"

Emily knew Brandon was still talking, but that's as far as she heard that sentence. Whatever his reasoning, Brandon continued to pitch ways of reuniting Liz and her phone, and for each one Ana responded with a reason why that was a bad idea. Any other time Emily might have pointed out with more than a little bit of arrogance that Ana was currently holding a small dog stolen from a gas station, and was surely herself in the running for Bad Idea of the Decade, but this time she was unable to even utter a syllable. Her jaw became locked in terror, and suddenly, instead of speeding down the highway in a midsize SUV, Emily had the sensation that she was plummeting down the first drop of a roller coaster.

Brandon must've caught a glimpse of her eyes in the rearview mirror, because she heard him yelling her name: "Emily? *Emily?* Are you okay? EMILY!"

By that time Brandon had followed her gaze out the back windshield, and slowly, haltingly, he turned around and stared down the highway behind them. He began to softly repeat a string of curses so quietly and with such slow determination that it almost sounded like he was reciting poetry or an ancient incantation of some kind.

Ana was completely fixated on Pickles, so she wasn't aware of what was happening until the entire car was bathed in red and blue light, and the sound of everything else was drowned out by sirens.

"Emily!" she shrieked. "What is happening?"

"It appears we've been caught," she said, and as she did, a strange sense of calm washed over her.

"What do you mean?" Ana was having trouble making sense of the events at hand.

"I mean, it looks as if we won't be making it to the party," said Emily.

"Of course we will," shouted Brandon. "Just step on it."

"Give me a break, Brandon." Emily said this evenly and quietly. It seemed to rattle Brandon that she was so even-keeled in the face of impending doom.

"Whatever you do, don't pull over!" he yelled.

"What, and add 'evading arrest' to the charges?" Emily asked. "Not a chance. Besides, he's already got my license plate. Even if I did floor it now, he'd have every patrol car in a ten-mile radius on our tail in thirty seconds." Emily signaled and pulled onto the shoulder of the road, slowing to a stop, then putting the car into park.

In the rearview mirror she saw a short stubby man with fingers like sausages step out of the cruiser, hitch up his pants, and walk slowly toward her window. She wasn't sure if she should dig out her registration and license now, or wait until he knocked on her window. She wasn't sure if she should try to text her father from the car, or wait and make him her one phone call at whatever jail they were taken to for the night. Emily wasn't sure of anything, really. Not anymore.

chapter 12

"License and registration."

It was a command, not a question. Emily pulled out her wallet, and got the registration and insurance card out of the glove compartment. Her dad had put all the documents together in a little canvas folder so she wouldn't have to dig for them. Emily smiled as she thought about her "hang loose" dad being organized about anything at all.

"Somethin' funny, young lady?" the cop asked. He had a shiny star pinned to his uniform that read ANDERS.

"No, sir," said Emily, wiping the smile off her face. "Is something the matter, officer?" The minute she said these words, she felt like she was in a movie from the 1950s.

"As a matter of fact there is."

Without another word, the cop turned back around and marched back to his cruiser. Emily could hear his radio squawking.

"Holy *shit*," hissed Brandon. "We are so *dead*."

Ana groaned and laid her head against the dashboard. "Go ahead," she muttered. "Say 'I told you so.'"

Emily didn't say a word. The officer was walking back toward the car.

"Step out of the car, please," he said sternly. "All of you."

"Should I bring the dog?" whispered Ana. Emily shot her a glance that said *no* in a very clear way, and unbuckled her seat belt. She'd never worn handcuffs before. She wondered what it would be like.

Once they were all standing on the shoulder of the road, Pickles began to bark incessantly inside Emily's car, and the officer introduced himself.

"I'm Sheriff Bud," he said. "I'd like to ask you a few questions."

Emily nodded.

"Where are you kids headed?"

"To a party." Ana blurted out.

"That right?" Sheriff Bud asked Emily.

Emily nodded.

"And did you stop for lunch today?"

"Yes! Yessir, we did." Brandon was practically panting. "We stopped for lunch at Rick's Diner and boy, oh, boy was it delicious, just the best food I've ever eaten for lunch. That Strawberry Tsunami they serve is just out of this world! Dyn-o-mite!" Emily looked up at Brandon, who was acting like he was on speed. She frowned at him, trying to silently telegraph that Bud was asking *her* the questions, so she should answer. Brandon and Ana were not helping by jumping in and trying to answer for her. It was coming across like they had something to hide.

After his soliloquy on the joys of Rick's Diner, Emily was sure that Brandon was going to get them all hauled in for questioning. Bud eyed Brandon and Ana, who kept fidgeting and clearing their throats and coughing. Finally, he turned back to Emily.

"I pulled you over because your license plate got sent through the system this afternoon. A couple of local idiots held Rick's up, and the owner of the diner said they escaped in your car." Bud looked from Emily to Ana, then over to Brandon. "Is that right?"

Emily waited for Ana and Brandon to jump in and spill the whole story, but both of them froze and stared at their feet. Emily looked at Brandon on her left, who shrugged, and Ana on her right, who ran a hand through her hair and suddenly acted as if her shoes were the most fascinating things she had ever laid eyes on.

Emily looked back at Bud and nodded. "Yes, sir. They did get away in our car." Brandon and Ana both turned and stared at her, their mouths hanging open. "But not because we wanted them to," Emily continued. "They had guns."

"You were eating in the diner when they came in?" Bud asked.

"Yes, sir," said Emily. "They grabbed the cash from the register and took us hostage for a little while."

"Did they hurt you?" Bud asked.

"No," said Emily. "Just scared us. They wanted to be dropped off, so we dropped them off."

"Where'd you do that?" asked Bud.

"At the Arco back at the last exit," said Emily.

"And you didn't think to call the police?" asked Bud.

"Well, I was just so shaken up," said Emily. "Plus, I didn't want to be accused of helping them rob the diner."

"I would've called, but one of them broke my phone," blurted Ana.

"I'm sorry to hear that," said Bud. "You all are lucky you got away from those morons when you did."

"You know who it was?" asked Brandon.

"Yeah, it's this couple of crazies used to go to high school not far from here. Hooked up back then and fancy themselves a modern-day Bonnie and Clyde." Bud lifted his hat and ran his hand through his thinning hair. "Course they never get away with much, but that wouldn't stop the prosecutor from pressing charges. It's just they always manage to give us the slip."

"Are we in trouble?" asked Emily. "I'm really sorry we didn't call the police."

"Nah," said Bud. "It's understandable. I imagine it was pretty traumatic to be held at gunpoint like that."

Emily nodded. Bud handed her a card.

"This here's my cell number," he said. "If you think of anything else that might be useful for me to know, give me a call. Otherwise, you kids have fun at your party, and be careful. Do not drink and drive—or you *will* be in a heap a trouble. I promise you that."

Once they were back in Emily's car and Sheriff Anders had pulled a U-turn through the highway's grassy median, no one spoke for several minutes. Finally, Brandon's voice broke the silence from the backseat.

"Hostage?" he said. "They took us hostage?" Then he started laughing. "Holy shit, Emily. How did you even keep a straight face?"

"I was terrified of being hauled away to prison," said Emily. "That *might've* helped a bit."

"What are we going to do with Liz's phone now?" asked Ana. She was holding Pickles in her arms like an infant.

"Well, one thing is for sure," said Emily. "We can't try to contact Liz or take it back to her. If the police already know it was them, we can't have any further contact with them *ever*. I say we throw it out the window in a mile or two and forget any of this ever happened."

"Amen. I second that motion," Brandon said.

Ana was quiet for a minute, but Emily could almost hear the wheels turning in her friend's head. Finally, Ana turned to Brandon with a mischievous smirk. "You know, there might be another option."

chapter 13

"Absolutely *not*." Brandon was adamant.

"Look, I'm just saying that we can probably beat Liz and Chestnut there," said Ana, "and they've never met the guys they're getting the goods from."

"I'm not sure that's really a plus for getting involved in the international drug trade," Emily said. "Besides, we don't even know where to go."

"Sure we do," Ana smiled slyly, holding up Liz's cell phone and waggling it back and forth in between her thumb and forefinger.

"NO!" Brandon bellowed from the backseat.

Emily laughed at him. "Wait. Let me get this straight. After everything else, *now* you're going to get all goody-two-shoes on us?"

"You guys," Brandon leaned so far over the front seat, he was practically sitting in between them. "We knew for sure that Liz and Chestnut had no bullets in their guns. We certainly *don't* know that about the assholes who are holding this cocaine."

"Oh, c'mon," said Ana. "Do you really think these people

can be so big time if they've agreed to go into business with a man named Chestnut?"

Brandon groaned. Emily was enjoying not being the person who was saying no for once. She'd felt like everybody's mom all day. Playing devil's advocate to make Brandon miserable was actually sort of fun.

"And this is their first time doing it," Emily reminded Brandon. "These guys we'd be picking up from have no idea what Liz and Chestnut are supposed to look like. It'd be super easy to pass ourselves off. You can be Chestnut and I'll be Liz."

"Yeah!" said Ana.

"Oh, give me a break," Brandon said. "How do you know they haven't seen pictures of Liz and Chestnut? And what about passwords or secret handshakes or some sort of code to let them know they've got the right people?"

"We'll just play stupid if they suspect anything," said Emily, and as she did, she wondered if she was teasing anymore. There was something about outsmarting small-time criminals that appealed to her. She was always just the uptight girl who paid attention to details to get good grades and for no other reason. Besides her GPA, what did she have to show for her fastidious nature and deliberate powers of observation? Nothing but a reputation for being uptight—a stone-cold bitch who needed to "loosen up" and "lighten up." What if she could prove once and for all that she was capable of marshaling these things everyone else saw as personality flaws to be assets. What if they could rip off some drug dealers and, at the same time, keep Liz and Chestnut from dragging poor little Artie into a life of danger from the drug cartel.

"And how, exactly, would we 'play stupid'?" demanded Brandon. "I mean, if they ask us for the password or something, are you just going to say, 'Oh! I'm sorry, we're not actually Liz and Chestnut after all!'? Because trust me, these guys will have guns with real bullets in them."

"Just don't tell them who you are first," said Ana.

"What?" Brandon was incredulous. "How do you think they're going to let us in if we don't pretend to be Liz and Chestnut?"

Ana shrugged. "I dunno. Just knock on the door and see how it goes. You can just ask for directions or something."

"Ask for directions? Like we're lost at a *random warehouse*?" Brandon ran his hands through his hair in frustration. "This is a bad, bad idea."

"No worse an idea than holding up a convenience store with Tweedle Dee and Tweedle Dumb," Emily said.

"What? That is not even *close* to the same thing."

"Sure it is," said Ana. "Close enough."

"Argh!" Brandon threw himself back against his seat.

"What's the address?" Emily asked. She was feeling like a superhero now.

"You can't be serious!" Brandon was getting really upset.

"Oh, c'mon, Mister You Only Live Once," Emily said. "Think of all the good we'd be doing."

"By stealing a shipment of cocaine?" Brandon's voice was jumping octaves now.

"Exactly," said Emily. "We'll go dump it in a river or flush it down a toilet or something. And *then* we'll have done a really good thing for humanity—not to mention Artie and Liz and Chestnut."

Brandon considered this. "You mean you wouldn't go try to sell it yourself?"

Ana started laughing. "Oh my God. Are you *loco*? Can you imagine this little white girl as a drug dealer?"

"Hey!" Emily said. "I *could* sell drugs. I'd probably be really good at it, actually. I have an attention to detail that makes me uniquely suited for avoiding capture while performing an illegal activity. However, no, I would never sell drugs."

"So . . . what's the point?" Ana asked. "I mean, if we showed up with that bag at the party, we'd probably be the most popular people on the planet."

"Not. An. Option." Emily used her no-nonsense voice. "The point is that we're having our *Thelma & Louise* day today."

"Our what?" Ana blinked at Emily like she was speaking Korean.

"Um, you *do* remember that *Thelma & Louise* does not end particularly well," Brandon said.

"I have one word for you," Emily said.

"What's that?" Brandon asked.

"YOLO."

"I was afraid of that," Brandon said with a sigh.

"You in?" Emily asked.

"Is there any way to stop you?" he asked.

"Probably not." Emily grinned into the mirror. "You gonna be my Chestnut?"

"Fine. But I'm dialing nine-one-one on my phone before we walk in and if anything even smells wrong, I'm hitting the call button."

"That's your exit," said Ana, pointing at the next off-ramp. "It's right around the corner."

Emily's heart was racing as she pulled off the highway, but there was a smile on her face. This *definitely* wasn't on the itinerary, but maybe that was a little bit okay.

chapter 14

The warehouse looked like it was about a mile long, and when Emily pulled into the parking lot, she wasn't exactly sure where to go. She drove slowly along the front of the building until they came to the far end and saw a door up three metal stairs. Appropriately, the door was painted powder white.

"Are we sure about this?" Brandon asked.

"Of course not," said Ana. "That's what makes it exciting!" She jumped out of the car, ran around to the driver's side, and pulled open Emily's door.

"What are you doing?" Emily hissed. "I wanted a few more minutes to go over details."

"Nah, just go for it," Ana said. "Gotta do it before you think too much about it." She pulled open Brandon's door too. "C'mon, you two. Quick! Like pulling off a Band-Aid."

Emily knew Ana was right, and it was too late to turn back now. If there were cameras or a window anywhere, they'd already been seen. She jumped out of the car and handed the keys to Ana. "You and Pickles are driving the getaway car. Be ready."

Ana winked. *"¡Estaremos listos!"*

Emily laughed. "You ready, Chestnut?" Brandon looked like he might be sick to his stomach. She grabbed his arm and pulled him up the stairs. "C'mon. What's the worst that can happen?"

"We'll be shot and killed?" he asked.

"Oh, please." Emily reached out to knock, but before her knuckles hit the door, it swung open.

To call the two men who stood in the doorway "large" would be to tragically understate the situation. Emily remembered how her dad had taken her to see some of the New York Jets defensive linemen who were making an appearance at the mall. She'd always thought of her father as a big muscular guy. He was six foot two, and naturally fit. To her he was basically He-Man—until she'd seen him next to those massive football players. And these guys in front of her now were even bigger. But as she stared up at them in their mirrored wraparound sunglasses, she almost started laughing because they were like caricatures of what a drug dealer's bodyguards were supposed to look like. They wore black T-shirts that strained against their massive muscles, faded blue jeans that came straight out of the early 90s, and both of them had shaved heads that seemed fused directly onto their shoulders, with no visible neck.

"Yeah?" one of them asked.

Emily swallowed her nervous laughter into a smile. She had to keep her cool and act like this was totally her element. Despite the ridiculous looks, these two could snap both her and

Brandon in half with one hand. "Here for the pickup," she said.

The guy who had greeted them glanced back at the mountain of a man standing behind him. Emily was still holding onto Brandon's arm, and she felt it tense up under her fingers. Out of the corner of her eye she saw that he was reaching into his front pocket, no doubt going for his phone to hit the call button like he promised he would. She quickly dug her fingernails into his arm.

"Ouch!" Brandon yelped. The guy turned back around.

"Oops!" giggled Emily, doing her best imitation of a carefree laugh. "Stepped on Chestnut's toe!" Inside her head, she heard a voice shouting *MAYDAY, MAYDAY*, but she tried to ignore it. They were already this far in. Nothing to do now but keep going.

"You're Chestnut?" The first guy asked. Emily began to wonder if the second one even possessed the power of speech. His neck, she thought, might be entirely made of muscle with no leftover space for vocal chords.

"Yep!" chirped Emily. "And I'm Liz." She thrust her hand out toward the guy who was talking to them. He looked down at it for a moment. "C'mon!" she teased him. "Don't leave me hangin'."

Slowly, the man reached out and took her hand with his gigantic meaty paw. Emily felt as if her arm was about to be swallowed by a hippo. As he shook her hand, the guy sized her up.

"I'm Ruff," he said, "and this is Scrappy. Ya'll are younger than I expected." He turned back to his silent partner. "Thought he wasn't using kids anymore."

Silent Scrappy shrugged.

"Let's go." Ruff dropped her hand and turned to lead the way into the warehouse.

Emily pulled Brandon along behind her, and they followed Ruff and Scrappy into the darkness. As her eyes adjusted to the low lighting, she saw rows and rows of boxes stacked to the ceiling on forklift pallets. There were aisles between the rows, and Scrappy led them to the very back row, then turned right and walked halfway down the length of the warehouse. As they walked, Emily felt her heart pounding, but also noticed that the warehouse seemed to be incredibly clean. She'd expected it to be dusty, or smell like old mildew like the laundry room in her aunt Mildred's basement, but it wasn't like she was up-to-date on the cleanliness rules of drug hideouts.

Just when Emily was beginning to wonder if they were being taken to their deaths, Scrappy stopped at a big plate-glass window in the back wall of the warehouse, where there appeared to be a bunch of offices. He rapped on the glass, and there was a buzz as the auto-lock on the door popped open. Scrappy held the door open and Ruff directed them into what looked to be a small office, complete with a desk and three folding chairs. A tiny man with long dark hair pulled into a ponytail was leaning against the desk. He had a beard with a white stripe down the center, and a thin pink scar stretched a broad arc across his left cheek.

Ruff indicated the folding chairs, and Emily and Brandon both took a seat. "This is Big Dog."

Emily could only stare. He was no taller than she was. In fact, if she'd been wearing the heels she'd packed for the party, she'd have a good three or four inches on him.

The tiny man smiled and hoisted himself onto the desk to sit. This effectively made him taller then they were while sitting in the folding chairs, but not by much. He leaned forward, his hands on either side of his legs. Emily noticed a gold pinky ring with a black onyx on his left hand.

"You must be Liz and Chestnut," he said with a smile. Emily was startled by his British accent. "I take it you've met my associates?"

"Yes, sir." Brandon answered, and Emily was both surprised and relieved to hear his voice.

"Excellent." Big Dog nodded at Scrappy, who lumbered through a door behind the desk and returned with a black rolling suitcase which he parked next to the desk. "Thank you, Scrappy. Now then, perhaps the two of you would join me for a cup of tea while we get to know one another for a moment?"

Even though he'd asked a question, something about the way he said this denoted that there was only one correct answer, and that was "Yes. Certainly." This was exactly what Emily said. Under any other circumstance, she might have giggled at this scene. Something about Big Dog's proper accent and demeanor, the way he called Scrappy and Ruff his "associates"—it was all sort of surreal. Still, there was something about this man that made Emily's blood run cold. She couldn't shake the feeling that even though he was pouring her a proper cup of perfectly brewed English tea in a bone china tea set with a lovely floral print, he'd just as easily snap his fingers and have Scrappy tear her limb from limb. The effect was chilling, and she could tell that Brandon felt it too by the way his cup clattered against his saucer when he sat it down after taking a sip.

Big Dog held the pinky finger with the ring very delicately away from this cup as he sipped the steaming tea and considered Brandon and Emily. "Well, Chestnut, you and Liz come very highly recommended."

Emily felt Brandon go tense. "Uh, yes . . . well, thank you. We're . . . pleased to have the opportunity to work with you." Emily kept her smile firmly in place.

"I must admit," said Big Dog, "that when I heard you were a team who'd met in high school I was under the impression that you were no longer . . . *in* high school." Emily saw his eyes narrow, and she decided to go for broke.

"Oh, you *charmer.*" She giggled at Big Dog, sliding her hand over Brandon's and intertwining their fingers. "You're too kind. My mother always told me to just say thank you when I received a compliment, so I'll simply say 'thank you.'"

Something about this seemed to please Big Dog, and he nodded slowly. "You must've been young when you had your son. How old is he again now?"

"Artie?" asked Emily. "Oh, he's just turned five. Yes, I was only fifteen." She slid her fingers from Brandon's hand up his arm and ruffled the hair at the back of his head. "He couldn't keep his hands off me."

"Do you have a picture of Artie?" Big Dog asked, his smile suddenly as cold as steel.

"A picture?" Emily tried to keep her voice from squeaking, but her throat was suddenly dry, and she quickly took a sip of her tea.

"I'd so love to see the little fellow." Big Dog calmly raised his cup to his lips and took a sip, but his eyes never left Emily's.

Emily was fairly certain her heart was about to either stop or explode. "Oh, you see . . . I don't really have anything on hand, so . . ."

"Here's your phone, babe."

Emily turned to see Brandon holding out a cell phone. *Liz's* cell phone. "Thanks, sweetie!" she said. Giggling, she turned to Big Dog and made a funny face. "I can be such an airhead sometimes. Thought I'd left it in the car." She brought the phone close to her so Big Dog couldn't see her hands shake. Quickly, she pulled up Liz's albums, flipped through the pictures until she came across one of Artie, then held the phone out to Big Dog with a smile.

Slowly, Big Dog placed his teacup back onto his saucer, set both down on the desk, then hopped down to come across the room to take the phone. He glanced down at the picture of Artie and smiled after a short pause. "He's quite a handsome young man," he said as he handed the phone back.

"Oh, he takes after his dad," Emily gushed as she handed the phone back to Brandon, then leaned over and pecked him on the cheek.

"Indeed," said Big Dog. He raised his eyebrows and nodded, then drained the last of his tea. "Well, we should let you be on your way then."

Big Dog motioned to Ruff, who wheeled the suitcase over to Brandon.

Emily fought the urge to grab Brandon's hand and race out of the room. Instead, she smiled at Big Dog and said, "It was a pleasure to meet you."

"Likewise." He smiled. Brandon nodded, and started rolling the suitcase toward the door. Emily was right on his heels, and as she held the door open so Brandon could roll the suitcase out into the warehouse, Big Dog's voice stopped her.

"We'll be here until seven p.m. We'll expect to see you back before then."

Emily froze, and felt Brandon do the same. Slowly, they both turned around.

"To-tonight?" Brandon stuttered.

"Well, naturally," Big Dog smiled. "You don't want to keep me waiting on my money overnight, do you, Chestnut?"

"Oh . . . uh, no. No, sir." Emily felt a drop of cold sweat trickle down her back. She didn't even know what Big Dog was talking about, and she allowed her mind to wander briefly to what fate exactly would befall her and Brandon if

Big Dog found out that she was planning to dump the suit-case of cocaine Brandon was holding into a toilet or a swimming pool. The thought was not pleasant.

"Excellent. So, you'll make the drop at Balducci's now, then bring the money back here as we agreed upon."

"Right. Yes, sir," Brandon said. "That's the plan. And we always stick to the plan." He gave Emily a pointed look when he said this, obviously referring to their complete inability to stick to a plan the entire day.

"And remember, for every minute after seven, you'll be docked $100 dollars from your one thousand dollar fee." Emily saw Brandon blink twice as this idea sunk in. "You understand? I don't like to wait."

"Yep." Brandon smiled. "Not a problem."

"Godspeed, Chestnut."

chapter 15

"Holy shit." Ana sped down the on-ramp back onto the highway. Pickles sat on her lap, his nose snuggled underneath a tiny paw.

"No kidding," Emily said. "Okay, this restaurant looks like it's about thirty miles away from the Steins' place." She had taken Liz's phone back from Brandon, who was currently lying down across the backseat practically hyperventilating. As Emily tapped at the screen of Liz's phone with her thumbs, she kept trying to talk Brandon down. "Brandon? You still with us? Need us to find you a paper bag to breathe into?"

"You're totally *loca*," Ana said. "I can't believe you pulled that off!"

"It was all Brandon." Emily leaned back over the seat and patted Brandon's arm. "Hey, mister. You okay?"

Brandon took a deep breath and sat up. "No, I am not okay. We are so dead."

"I agree it's not ideal," said Emily, "but thanks to you, we may survive."

"Thanks to *me*?" Brandon yelped. "I looked like a complete moron in there. I totally almost got us *killed*."

"Um, no. Actually, you totally saved my ass in there," said Emily. "I mean, that moment with Liz's phone? *Brilliant.* I didn't even know you had it on you. I was totally stuck."

"That doesn't solve the problem that he *knows* we're not Liz and Chestnut," Brandon said.

"Nah," said Emily. "I think he was testing us. I think he might have suspected something when he saw how young we are, but we pulled it off."

"How can you be sure?" Brandon asked.

Ana laughed. "Well, you do have a suitcase of cocaine in the backseat."

"Which probably means you shouldn't be driving like a maniac," Emily said. "And here." She reached over and plucked Pickles out of Ana's lap, snuggling him onto her own. "I think Pickles can stay with me for a while so you can stay focused on the matter at hand, a.k.a. *driving.*"

"Oh wow. *Right.*" Ana let her foot off the gas a bit. "I guess I was driving pretty fast. So, does this mean we're *not* throwing the cocaine in a river or flushing it down a toilet?"

"NO!" Emily and Brandon both shouted at the same time.

"Jeez, okay, okay. You don't have to yell at me," Ana said.

"Sorry." Emily reached out and touched her friend's arm. "We're a little bit . . . on edge."

"Scarier then you thought, huh?" said Ana.

"Yeah, just a touch."

"So, what *is* the plan now?" Brandon asked.

"We're going to Balducci's to get this giant amount of

cocaine that could land us in a federal penitentiary for the rest of our lives *out* of my car." She wasn't really sure when she'd decided that this was the new plan, maybe sometime between leaving the office and leaving the warehouse, but dumping the cocaine suddenly seemed like a bad idea. Like it could easily backfire if someone saw them, or caught them, trying to dispose of an entire suitcase. Not to mention what Big Dog might do if he had more information about them, the *real* them, than they thought.

"But then we're going to have thousands of dollars in a bag or suitcase or whatever in the car, and a bloodthirsty gangster on our tail."

"Not if we take him the money," said Emily.

"Wait, but I thought you were the one who was all about taking these drugs out of circulation," said Brandon.

"Yeah," Ana chimed in. "What happened to being all Robin Hood and stuff?"

"Actually, Robin Hood robbed from the rich to give to the poor, so I'm not sure that analogy really makes much sense," Emily said.

Ana just blinked with confusion.

Emily sighed. "All I'm saying is that we can't keep a suitcase full of cocaine in the car. I mean, what else can we do? It's not like we have a place to dump it along the way without just tossing it out the car, which could lead to a *ton* of other problems. And we can't take it and dump it at the Steins', because they would get in trouble and everyone would know what we did. And we don't have anywhere else to sell it, right? And if we even try any of these things, Big Dog and his *associates* could come after us.

"We're so dead," Brandon moaned, thumping his head against the front seat. "So, *so* dead."

"Brandon! *Please!*" Emily yelled. "I need you to pull it together. You were a rock star back there. You got Scarface to tell us the plan, even though we should've known it already. He even told us the restaurant. We've got everything we need because of you. You and Liz's cell. So pull yourself together!"

Brandon stopped banging his head on the seat.

"Thank you. Now, like I said, it's not like we're going to sell the drugs ourselves. We don't have anywhere to take them, and even if we did . . . we're three kids from the suburbs. Big Dog might've believed that we're running transport, but do you think anyone else would believe that we're selling? And we don't even know *how* to sell cocaine. What do you even package it in?"

"Bricks," Ana said. "Or baggies. At least that's what happens on *CSI.*"

"I'm not about to risk my life on a fact from a TV show," Emily said. "We're going to take the stuff to the restaurant, get the proper amount of money, bring that back to Big Dog at the warehouse, and then we can each walk away with about $325 in our pockets."

"Wouldn't it be more like $333?" Ana asked.

"You think I'm not deducting the gas fee for this?" Emily asked.

Brandon sighed loudly. "Okay, fine. I see your point."

Emily nodded. "Thank you. Ana?"

"Yeah, yeah," Ana said. "We've started some kind of cartel. I've got it."

"Look, I know this wasn't the plan," Emily said. "And I know I'm usually the one shouting about sticking to the plan . . . so I take full responsibility for this detour, and everything we're going through. That's why I want to fix it. I know it's my fault."

"Huh?" Ana glanced at her. "How is it your fault?"

Emily took a deep breath. "I just wanted to do something different. Something spontaneous. I wanted to stop being the stick-in-the-mud. The one always following the rules. You guys are always telling me "you only live once," and I wanted to, I don't know, take that to heart and do something I never would do on a normal day. I wanted to make today special."

"Getting involved with three thugs and a suitcase of cocaine is your definition of 'special'?" Brandon asked.

"Remind me not to hire you to set up my next party," Ana muttered.

"You know what I mean," Emily said with a sigh. "Anyway, the plan seemed to make a lot more sense before we actually *met* Big Dog and he served us tea."

"He served *tea*?" Ana asked with disbelief.

"No scones, though," Brandon put in.

"And don't be fooled," Emily said. "He might've been tiny,

and he might've served us tea, but I feel like this guy was the real deal. It wasn't anything he did specifically—he didn't do much of anything really, but you could totally get the sense that this guy had *been* places, you know?"

Brandon nodded. "And he had the scar to prove it."

"Sooo . . . what about Liz and Chestnut, then?" Ana asked after a moment.

"What about them?" Emily asked. "They'll be able to take care of themselves, right?"

"Well, I was thinking . . . ," she said slowly. "They're going to get back to their car eventually, right? And then they're going to make their way to the warehouse and have a little chat with Super Pup."

"Big Dog," Brandon said.

"Whatever. What are we going to do when they get to Big Dog *before* we get back with the money. Aren't they all going to assume that we just stole a suitcase of cocaine from them?"

"Damn." Brandon sank back against the seat. "She's right. We can't go back there. We're not going to make it, and I doubt they'll believe that this was all a big misunderstanding when we stroll up again."

Emily took a deep breath, realizing that she'd severely miscalculated. "We're totally screwed."

chapter 16

Emily spent the next ten miles explaining to Brandon that their only hope was to get to the restaurant before Liz and Chestnut got to Big Dog's warehouse and Big Dog called his contacts at Balducci's. "That way we can *maybe* get the money back to them and even though we would've fooled them, they might not absolutely hate us since the job would've gotten done."

Brandon wanted to call the police.

"We are not calling the police." Emily was adamant. "How are we going to explain all of this cocaine?"

"We just tell them the truth," Brandon said.

"And what?" asked Emily. "Just hope that they understand and let us go?"

"Well, yeah," said Brandon.

"Oh my God." Emily held her head in her hands. She felt like she was going to start crying. After a couple of deep breaths, she tried again. "If they find the cocaine in my car, they will impound it, no questions asked. And if they impound my car, we will—"

"Never make it to the party!" Ana shouted, only she said "party" like "par-TAAAY!" as if she were three shots in on a beach over spring break with MTV filming from the sidelines.

"Are you *kidding me?*" Brandon said. "This is still about the *party?* Oh my sweet Jesus, you have *got to let it go.*"

"This isn't about the party!" Emily shouted.

"This is *totally* about the party," Ana said, shaking her head. "This whole *day* is about the party. You know it, Emily. I know it. Brandon, even you know it, though right now you're acting like Emily and being the goody-two-shoes, and I don't even know why because we *both* know that you're not."

Emily and Brandon were both silent.

"Here's the deal," Ana said. "It doesn't make sense, at this point, to go to the police. That'll cause more trouble than it's worth, and there's no saying we would get out of it. We made the choice to go to the warehouse, and that puts us at fault. So no police. Not now.

"What makes this all about the party is that the party is what got us here. The idea of the party. The fun. The freedom. We're in this situation because we wanted to get there, and if we don't get there, if we don't *party*, then what is any of this for? So we're going to the party, no matter what."

"And what about the drugs?" Brandon asked after a pause.

"We're taking the suitcase to Balducci's."

"And then taking the money back to the warehouse?" Emily asked to confirm.

"Nope."

Both Emily and Brandon gaped.

"Look, our original plan was to throw the cocaine in a river, or a pond, or flush it down the toilet after, I don't know, a thousand flushes. But then we don't get anything, and we possibly get caught because of the amount of time it would take."

"But what about taking the money back to the warehouse?" Brandon asked.

Ana shook her head. "Bad idea. We could only do that if we were sure we'd make it back before the real Liz and Chestnut made it there in the first place, and we can't be sure about that. And while we could hope they'd be understanding and let us go because the job got done, we can't be sure of that, either. So the only thing we can be sure of is that we can get the drugs to the restaurant, and then get out without anyone knowing who we are or where we came from. Then we're in the wind, and richer for it."

Brandon nodded. "Maybe even thirty grand richer. Each."

Emily whirled around and looked at him. "You think there's *ninety thousand dollars'* worth of cocaine in there?"

Brandon shrugged. "Sure. It's heavy as hell."

"*Dios mio,* how would you know that?" Ana asked.

"You know, *CSI,*" Brandon said. "*Law & Order.*"

"*Ay!*" Ana shouted. "That's not helpful. You have no idea how much is in there. But it doesn't even matter. They'll know how much to give us."

"What if they rip us off?"

"Do we care? Whatever they give us is more than we had before."

"I still don't feel great about this," Emily said. Though

she'd set this whole thing in motion, and though she wanted to break out of her shell and do something crazy for once, the adrenaline was starting to run out and her usual careful self was starting to return.

"Here's an option," Ana said. "We can Robin Hood it."

"Huh?" Brandon leaned forward. "Give the cocaine to the poor? I mean, I'll admit that they might know what to do with it better than we do, but I don't know if promoting drug use is really the way to go, Ana."

"No," Emily said, shaking her head. "She's talking about the money."

Ana grinned. "*Exactamente*. The money."

"We can take the money we make from the cocaine and give it to charity," Emily said. "We could do it anonymously. That'll make the whole thing better. Sort of."

Brandon shrugged. "I guess that's not a *terrible* idea," he said. "But what's to guarantee that Big Dog won't hunt us down and kill us?"

"There's no guarantee that Ana's not going to kill us on this road," Emily said, watching as the street and other cars sped by. "Besides, I'm not really sure he'll be able to track us down. And at least this way, if we give it to charity, this whole thing wouldn't have been a waste. We'll be doing good."

"Kinda," Brandon said.

Ana whooped. "For charity!"

Brandon nodded and looked at Ana. "Nice thinking, babe." There was an awkward silence for a moment as the word "babe" floated down over them like a heavy woolen blanket.

"Babe?" Emily asked, smirking.

Ana kept her eyes straight ahead but made duck lips, and Emily saw her eyebrow twitch upward like she'd scored a point or something. Brandon immediately started coughing and sputtering and explaining it was just a habit and finally Emily turned up the music, turned around, and put a finger to her lips.

He got the hint and shut up.

As Brandon tried to recover from the "babe" moment, Emily tossed Liz's phone into the cup holder and pulled out her own. When she checked her e-mail, she had twelve new messages, all from Kyle. The subject lines were all some variation on "I'm sorry," or "I want you back," or "I miss you." The most recent one was just the word "PLEASE."

As she scrolled down the list of unread messages with her thumb, a wave of something she could only identify as nostalgia washed over her. That was the thing about Kyle: As annoying as he could be, he was so freaking cute. At times when she was exhausted, like now, he had this way of snuggling up behind her on the couch or on her bed and wrapping his whole body around hers. That was all she wanted to feel at this moment. Nobody had ever held her like he did.

Or drove you quite as nuts as he did.

The thought ricocheted through her brain just as her thumb was about to tap open the first new e-mail from Kyle. She dropped her phone next to Pickles in her lap like a hot rock, and took a deep breath. This was always her internal struggle with Kyle: Her body would let down the guard when she was tired. Luckily, her brain would kick in and remind her not to do stupid things like read all of his e-mails when she was exhausted and stressed-out. While part of her ached to be held the way only Kyle had been able to, she knew that after five minutes, he'd start blowing in her ear or tickling her or asking her if she wanted to take a bong rip, and from that point it was all downhill.

Emily knew that she was in a fragile emotional state at the moment and that if she read all the apologies from Kyle, all she'd be able to see was his perfect lips and his bright blue eyes. Right at this moment if she read the sweet promises he'd made to change, she'd feel like saying yes—even though her brain was shouting *Mayday! Mayday!*

She'd been around and around with Kyle. He always promised to change things about himself that he'd never be able to, and always wanted her to change the things about herself that, well, made her . . . *her.* Yeah, so she was never going to want to get stoned and watch the X-Games all day on a Saturday. No, she was not going to cut AP chemistry so she could get drunk and play laser tag. In the end, it was bad that Kyle liked those things. It didn't mean he was a *bad* guy. It just meant that he wasn't *her* guy. It was a choice between good and better. There had to be somebody out there who was more suited to her. She deserved to be able to discuss the books she read with somebody. She deserved a guy who liked indie films and didn't wrinkle his nose when she ate sushi, or who would suggest that they volunteer for a Saturday at Habitat for Humanity.

So, no, Emily decided. Right at this second, she would *not* read Kyle's e-mails. She scratched under Pickles's chin and he curled up in her lap, quickly sinking into a calm sleep. That's when Emily realized Ana was laughing—at something Brandon had said to her. They'd been talking while Emily was checking her messages, and Emily realized that, shockingly, she hadn't heard them arguing at all. In fact, they seemed to be cracking jokes about a movie they'd both seen recently. This was truly intriguing because during the year that they dated, Emily couldn't remember a time when they had agreed upon a single movie they'd ever gone to together. In fact, they'd pretty much fought about everything from restaurants to reality shows. Now, as Emily watched, they actually seemed to be enjoying each other's company. Actually, it was beyond enjoyment. They seemed to be genuinely fond of each other.

"What?" Ana's voice broke into Emily's thoughts.

"Huh?" she jumped, startled. "Oh, nothing."

"You okay?" asked Brandon.

"I'll be better when we get the suitcase of drugs out of the backseat," she said.

"Well, you're in luck, *mamacita*. This is the exit." Ana eased the car up the ramp, and before Emily was truly ready, they were pulling into the parking lot of Balducci's.

chapter 17

Balducci's Pizzeria was in a strip mall, and as Emily opened the door, she half expected to see Tony Soprano and his entire family eating a slice and casually cursing at one another over beers and sodas. Instead, the most beautiful woman she'd ever seen was wiping down menus at the hostess stand. Her skin was the color of a vanilla latte and seemed to be lit from within. She had glossy black hair that hung in a short blunt cut right at her chin. And when she saw Emily, she smiled like a movie star.

"Welcome to Balducci's. Table for three?"

Emily glanced around the room. It was deserted except for the hostess, a bartender refilling the ice wells with a giant bucket, and two men nursing beers at the bar. One of them was tall and thin and wearing a fedora, which, under the circumstances, seemed somehow ridiculous. "Actually . . ." Emily's voice trailed off. She realized she wasn't sure how to broach the topic now that they were standing at the drop-off point. What was she supposed to say? *We're here with your cocaine!* She took a deep breath and smiled, then tried again. "We're here to make a delivery." She turned to where Brandon and Ana were standing behind her. Ana had Liz's cell phone in her hand, and Brandon was pulling the black suitcase.

"I'm Nina," the hostess said. She glanced down at the suitcase and took it in without even the slightest flicker of concern. "We've been expecting you. Follow me to your table."

Nina led them to a booth in the back. Once they were seated, she brought each of them a glass of water. "I'll be right back with Frank."

As they watched Nina walk toward the men at the bar, Brandon leaned in and whispered, "These guys are total mafia."

Emily rolled her eyes as she saw Nina indicate their table to the man in the hat, who appeared to be in no hurry to leave his beer. "Oh, c'mon. Don't you think a *fedora* is a little . . . ?"

"What?" asked Brandon.

"I dunno," Emily said. "On the nose? I mean, a pizza parlor, a fedora; what's next? A production number from *Guys & Dolls?*"

Ana giggled at this, but Brandon just said, "Look, stereotypes exist for a reason."

Emily guessed that he would've said more, except both of the men from the bar were walking toward them.

"Welcome to Balducci's." They guy in the fedora literally tipped his hat. Emily had to fight the urge to look around for a hidden camera. "I'm Frank. You must be Chestnut," he said to Brandon, then looked back and forth between Emily and Ana.

"I'm Liz," Emily said, raising a hand in a small wave.

"Ah, yes," said Frank. "This is my brother, Vito." Vito was about as wide as Frank was tall.

"Youse got something for us?" asked Vito, his Jersey accent so thick Emily wondered if he was pretending.

"Right here." Brandon rolled the suitcase out from under the table, and Vito took the handle.

"Be right back," said Vito.

As Vito rolled the suitcase away from the table, Frank motioned for Nina to come back. "We got fresh pie in the oven. Tell Nina what you'd like to drink."

"Oh, I don't think we have time to eat." Emily was creeped out by this entire arrangement. All she could think about was Liz and Chestnut pulling up to the warehouse and the look on Big Dog's face. It could happen at any moment, and she didn't want to be sitting around eating pizza when the call came from Big Dog that Frank and Vito should feel free to take them all out back. "We really need to get back on the road." She gave Frank as sincere a smile as she could.

"I insist." Frank tipped his fedora again and followed Vito out of the room.

Nina reappeared. "What may I bring you to drink?" she asked. "And is pepperoni okay with everyone?"

Brandon ordered a beer and, to Emily's surprise, no one asked him for an ID. Then again, they'd just delivered a suitcase of cocaine. Following liquor laws probably wasn't something she had to worry about.

Nina brought out the pizza, and once again Emily was

amazed at how much Brandon could eat (a) after all the food he'd had in the last few hours, and (b) under the circumstances. She'd felt like she was about to barf since they'd gotten to the warehouse.

"Are you okay?" Ana whispered as she pulled a piece of pizza onto her plate.

"Oh, fine," said Emily. "Just being forced to hang around eating pizza while the men playing mobster in the back weigh the drugs I brought them."

"I don't think they're *playing* mobster," said Brandon around a mouthful of pizza. He took the last swig of his first beer and caught Nina's eye. He waived the empty bottle in her direction with a smile, and she signaled the bartender for another. "I think they are full-on *mafiosos*."

"I just hope they hurry the hell up," said Ana. "This place is stressing me out and I do *not* want a stress breakout now."

"This is our last stop," said Emily. "The second they give us that money, we are heading to that party. Do not pass Go. Do not collect two hundred dollars."

"Oh, youse collectin' more than two hundred dollars." Vito had appeared behind Nina. She set down a beer for Brandon, and Vito wheeled a smaller black suitcase back under the table. "Product looks good as promised. Give Big Dog our regards."

"We certainly will," said Emily. She started to get up, but Vito placed a giant catcher's mitt of a hand on her shoulder. "Stay for a while," he said. When he smiled she could see he had a gold tooth. "Let Chestnut here finish his beer. You ladies want anything? It's on the house."

"Thanks, but we'd better get going," said Emily. "Have to get this money back to Big Dog."

Vito finally moved his hand to rub his stomach as he roared with laughter. "That Big Dog, he don't like to wait, eh? Looks like youse found this out." He wiped a tear from his eye. "Tell him Vito says he's a dirty mutt."

This prompted another fit of laughter from Vito. Emily slid out of the booth and motioned to Brandon, who was chugging the second beer. He finished and put the bottle on the table, then slid out of his side of the booth. Ana followed quickly, wrapping a piece of pizza in a napkin, and heading for the door. Brandon followed her, rolling the small suitcase of what Emily presumed was cash. Emily brought up the rear.

They were so close to being back in the car with thousands of dollars that every step she took felt like a victory. This handoff had gone more smoothly than she had ever dared to hope. Emily realized she wasn't sure what she had expected, but a kind hostess and free pizza had not been the way she'd envisioned it going down. She'd pictured tommy guns from the 1930s and men in white spats. Basically, any gangster movie ever.

At the front of the restaurant Ana pushed open the front door, and as she began to step over the threshold they heard a voice boom from behind them:

"Aren't you forgetting something?"

Emily froze. In front of her, Brandon and Ana turned around first. What Emily saw on their faces made her heart sink. She was certain, without even looking, that Frank had pulled a gun on them. Slowly she turned around and caught sight of the man in the fedora standing by the door that led to the kitchen at the very end of the bar.

He was not holding a gun.

He was holding Artie.

Vito stood next to them, glaring at Emily. "How's youse gonna fuhgit yer own kid?"

Emily's terror was complete. She had no snappy comeback. Her throat was closing off a little at a time. Her tongue was a desert. Had these men been holding Artie as collateral for the deal? Had Liz known this? Had Chestnut? Could they really not have mentioned this? Could they have been okay with this plan? How could they knowingly have allowed their son to be kept in the company of these men while they were out robbing restaurants and gas stations?

And how would she explain the fact that Artie would not recognize her or Brandon? He would never go anywhere with them. Their cover was officially blown. She glanced back at Brandon. His eyes widened as if to say, *I got nothing.*

Emily briefly considered running out of the restaurant and jumping into her car. It would've been the fastest choice: just run. But something in her wouldn't let her do it. She couldn't bring herself to leave Artie with these men. His fine brown hair was straight and longish, his bangs cut straight across his forehead, his cheeks still a little chubby, and a perfect dollop of freckles across his nose. He was even cuter in real life than he had been in the picture on Liz's phone.

After what seemed like an eternity but was only a few seconds at most, Emily took a hesitant step forward. "Hey, Artie!" she said, a smile covering the pit of fear churning in her stomach. She waited for a moment, bracing herself for the certain look of fear or confusion on Artie's face, for the moment when he blurted out, "Who are *you*?"

It never came.

Instead, Artie wiggled down out of Frank's arms and did something so surprising, if she hadn't grabbed the hostess stand, Emily might've fallen down.

A huge smile lit up Artie's face, and he threw open his arms, running toward her, all the way down the length of the restaurant. As he did, he yelled out a single word, a word that Emily decided was the sweetest sound in the English language. A word that may well have saved her life:

"Mommy!"

chapter 18

"Are you fucking *kidding me*?" Brandon was whisper-shouting. "Now we've got a *five-year-old in the car?*"

"*Hey!* Watch your language, potty mouth." Ana wagged a finger at Brandon, who threw his arms up in the air.

"Calm down," Emily said. Brandon continued his rant unabated.

"I mean a *dog* was bad *enough*. But now we've *kidnapped a child?* How could this day possibly get any *worse?*"

"It could be raining," Ana muttered.

They were standing next to the car in a dry ditch, filled with tall grasses and weeds. Emily had driven as slowly as she could out of the parking lot of Balducci's, then down the service road along the highway for about a mile before pulling over and convening a meeting with Ana and Brandon. She'd left Artie in the backseat with Pickles, who was curled up on Artie's lap already fast asleep.

"Actually, it's worse than rain," Brandon sputtered. "This isn't water falling from the sky. *This?* Is a *shit storm*. This is a *hurricane of calamity*. What the *hell* are we supposed to do now?"

Emily ran a hand through her hair. "Look, I never would have gone through with this whole pickup thing if I'd known that Liz and Chestnut were putting Artie in danger."

"Ya *think?*" Brandon was red in the face. He took a deep breath and walked around in a circle. "Okay, so can we please call the police now?"

Emily shook her head. "No. I mean, not yet."

"Oh? Not yet?" Brandon was mocking her. "What, do we need to have a pony with *wings* in the car along with the stolen dog and kidnapped child before we consider this a *crisis?*"

"We can call Chestnut," Emily said. "We'll just use Liz's phone and give him a call and sort all of this out. We can hand over Artie. We can hand over the cash, for all I care." At this point, Emily just wanted the day, and the experience, to be over. "Okay?"

"Not okay," Ana said, shaking her head. "First of all, don't you think Liz would've used Chestnut's phone to call hers if he actually had one."

"We don't know that," Brandon said quickly. "Come on, let me see the phone."

"Well, you know ... that's the other thing," Ana said as she chewed her lip. "I sort of, kind of, maybe don't have the phone anymore."

Emily and Brandon both gawked at her.

"What do you mean?" Emily asked. "How can you not have the phone anymore? We haven't done anything."

"I'm not really sure," Ana said. "I'm guessing I left it on the table at the restaurant." She held up her slice of pizza. "All of this stress-eating has made me forgetful."

"Okay, fine," Brandon said. "The one possible plan we had is no longer viable, meaning the only solution now is to actually *call the police.*"

Emily shrugged. She felt defeated. She'd tried to let loose, to make things fun and carefree, and look where that had gotten her. Nowhere good, that was for sure. If she could turn back the clock . . . but it didn't even matter. There was no use thinking that way, because they were already in a situation, and there wasn't any way they could fix it by going into the past. There wasn't a time-travel option. So they had to work with what they had, now, in the present, decide what to do.

And there was really only one thing to do after being involved in an armed robbery, dognapping, drug mule-ing, and kidnapping.

Without saying anything, she motioned to the car, then walked around to the driver's side and slid behind the wheel. Once Ana and Brandon were both inside and the doors were shut, she slowly reached for her phone.

"Who're you calling?" Artie asked from the backseat, where he was seated next to Brandon.

"The police," Emily said. "We have to get you home."

"Mom and Dad probably aren't there anyway," he said. Pickles was in his lap and he seemed more concerned about the small dog's tattered collar than he did his parents' whereabouts.

"Hey, Artie?" Emily said as she twisted in her seat to look at the boy. "Back in the restaurant, why did you call me 'Mommy'?"

"Well, you looked like you were in trouble," he said. "And I expected my mom to be there, but since she wasn't, and you were, I guessed that she sent you to get me instead. But I didn't want to get you in trouble."

"In trouble?"

He nodded. "Yeah. Mom and Dad are robbers, you know? So sometimes they have to work with bad guys, and if the bad guys knew you were the wrong people, then you would've been in trouble. Right?"

"Well . . . yeah, I suppose," Emily said. She couldn't argue with the logic, though she was surprised, flabbergasted even, that a five-year-old had been able to come to that conclusion so quickly and efficiently.

"So did my mom and dad send you?" he asked.

"Kind of," Emily said. "We were going to call them, but we don't have their number . . ."

"Oh, that's all right," Artie said. "We can just go see Buck and Blanche."

"Who're Buck and Blanche?" Ana asked.

"Do we even want to know?" Brandon mumbled as he stared out the window.

"They're my grandparents," Artie said happily. "Sometimes I stay with them while Mom and Dad are doing jobs. It was supposed to be like that today, but I think Dad made a bad deal, and that's when they had to take me to that restaurant, Balducci's, to leave me there. As collateral."

"Why do you know that word?" Brandon asked with obvious disbelief.

Artie seemed to think for a moment, then shrugged. "Must've heard someone say it."

"So, Buck and Blanche," Emily asked as she turned on the car. "Any chance you know where they live?"

Artie laughed. "Of course I do." He spouted out the address. "Mom and Dad always say that if there's ever trouble, I should find a good adult and get to Buck and Blanche's as soon as possible."

"A good adult?" Ana asked.

Artie nodded. "Not like the people at Balducci's. People like you guys."

Emily glanced at Ana, who shrugged, and then punched the address into the GPS. "Well, I guess we're off to see Buck and Blanche."

Artie cheered. "Everything's going to be great. I can tell."

Emily just shook her head. At this point, she wasn't convinced anything would be great ever again.

chapter 19

The house Emily pulled up in front of was small, but had a long front porch with a porch swing at one end, and several old wooden rocking chairs at the other. A woman with gray hair pinned up into a French twist opened the front door as Emily pulled into the driveway. She was tall, and Emily quickly noticed that she was wearing bright red high heels, boot-cut jeans, and a leather jacket that looked like it came straight off a Paris runway.

"Are you lost?" the woman called out.

"Blanche!" Artie was out of the car in a second, racing across the front yard before leaping to the woman to give her a hug around her waist.

The woman, Blanche, gave Artie a warm hug in return, then turned to the others with obvious suspicion. "Who are you, and what are you doing with my grandson?"

Emily got out of the car slowly, not really sure how to explain. Ana and Brandon trailed behind her as they approached the house, stopping at the bottom of the porch steps. Emily held out her hand to shake Blanche's, but the older woman didn't make any move to reciprocate, so Emily let her hand fall to her side.

"They picked me up," Artie said. "I was at a pizza place."

Blanche's eyes narrowed, then she untwined Artie from around her waist and said, "Go on inside and find Buck. I think he's down in the basement watching TV."

Artie nodded and started to go inside, but then stopped and let out a loud whistle. In a second, Pickles was at his feet, hopping around as they both trekked inside. Blanche barely even blinked at the dog.

Once Artie was gone, Emily decided to try again.

"So . . . it's all kind of a funny story," she said.

Blanche slipped her hand into her jacket pocket and pulled out a long slender cigarette, which she lit with a sleek silver lighter. She inhaled deeply, and then let the smoke issue slowly from her lips. She took another slow draw, then said, "Let me guess. Artie's parents somehow roped you into running an errand that resulted in unexpected free babysitting for them, and maybe a bad deal for you."

"Well . . . not exactly," Emily said. "I don't really know how to explain."

"I'll do it." Brandon strolled to the car and quickly pulled out the black suitcase, which he brought back to the porch and dropped next to Blanche unceremoniously. He tugged on the zipper and popped open the bag, revealing stacks and stacks of bills. Hundred-dollar bills.

"Well, would you look at that," Blanche said slowly, though her facial expression said that she wasn't all that impressed and had seen much more in her life. "Well." She took two more long drags on her cigarette, then delicately put it out on an ashtray that rested on the porch railing. "Why don't you collect that and come on inside. I'll make coffee."

Inside, Emily was somewhat surprised to see that the house was fresh, modern, and well put together. Each room had the look of an interior design catalog, with not one item out of place. The kitchen was especially put together, and she, Brandon, and Ana simply stared as Blanche bustled around, getting a fancy, expensive coffee machine brewing before setting out four mugs.

While the coffee machine sizzled and spurted, Blanche moved to the hall and called down to the basement, telling Buck and Artie to come on up to get something to eat.

"I don't suppose you know whether he had pizza at that parlor?" she asked.

Emily shook her head. "Not sure."

"Well, then!"

Emily, Brandon, and Ana all jumped when the voice boomed behind them, seeming to shake everything in the room. Emily turned to see a man with a salt-and-pepper beard and black horn-rimmed glasses stroll into the kitchen. He was taller than Brandon, and just as well put together as Blanche, with black slacks, a white shirt, and an unbuttoned vest.

"What's going on in here?" he asked, giving Emily, Brandon, and Ana a broad smile.

"That's what we're in the process of figuring out," Blanche

said. The coffee machine dinged, and she got to work pouring out cups. "Buck, pull that cheese and meat plate out of
the fridge."

Emily frowned at Ana and Brandon when she saw the full-
fledged antipasti platter that Buck pulled from the state-of-
the-art refrigerator and set on the island counter. It was only
a moment before she and her friends were seated on wooden
stools, sipping rich, hot coffee, and eating artisan cheeses and
cured meats.

"So lay it on me," Buck said. "What's going on? What did
my crackpot of a son and his wonky wife get into this time?"

Brandon and Ana both looked at Emily, and she sighed.
It was just like them to make her the leader of the group now,
when everything was about to come to light.

"Well, it was all one big misunderstanding, in a way,"
Emily started. She then took a deep breath and went through
the whole story, or at least the broad strokes. Eventually
she got to the part of their day when they were surprised by
Artie's presence at Balducci's. "Then he told us about you, and
that's how we ended up here," she finished.

"I can see how things got out of control," Blanche said.
She'd finished her coffee and was pouring herself, and everyone else, a second cup.

"I do have one question, though," Buck said from his place
at the side of the room, where he was leaning against a wall.
"There were lots of opportunities for you to stop along the
way. And lots of moments where you made the choice that

put you on this crazy path." He rubbed his chin and straightened his glasses.

"Just . . . in-the-moment decisions," Emily said slowly, not sure how else to answer.

Buck's eyes narrowed, and a smirk crossed his face. "Maybe," he said. "But I think there's more than that going on here. Don't you, Blanche?" Blanche laughed. "Oh, c'mon, Buck. It's written across her face plain as day. All three of 'em got bit bad."

"Bit?" asked Ana.

"By the crime-spree bug!" boomed Buck. "C'mon now. Didn't you all feel the thrill of your hearts pounding just a bit when you were pulling the wool over Stanley?"

"Stanley?" asked Brandon.

"Oh, hell, did you really think his name was Big Dog?" Blanche cackled. "That small-time asshole has been trying to build an empire since back when Buck and I were in the capering business."

"Wait," said Emily. "You two were . . . ?"

"Criminals?" asked Buck. "Yessiree, Bob. And good ones too. None of this small-time crap that Chestnut goes in for. Trained him better than that."

"Trained him?" asked Brandon. "You mean you showed him how to rob people?"

"Nah—not people. Banks. After closing time." Blanche beamed with pride. "We cracked safes."

"No guns, no drugs," said Buck.

"And certainly no diners in broad daylight," sighed Blanche. "That boy's gonna have to spend a decade in federal prison before he learns his lesson."

"Should just lock 'em both in the basement," roared Buck. "Least that way they'd be easier to visit."

"So you only robbed banks?" asked Ana.

"Yep. Federally insured money. Victimless crime," said Blanche. "Course that's all over now."

"How come?" asked Brandon.

"Well, mainly because we decided to quit while we were ahead," said Buck. "But also 'cause technology has made it impossible. It's a rare bank vault that still has an old-fashioned combo lock."

"And the cameras," Blanche moaned. "Might as well be Hollywood. They've got those buildings wired six ways to Sunday now."

"But it was fun while it lasted," said Buck.

"And lucrative," said Blanche.

"And not half as dangerous as it is now." Buck nudged the suitcase full of cash with his foot. "So what's your plan here? What's the next move?"

Emily shrugged. "Well, since Artie was involved and Big Dog—Stanley, I guess?—is sure to have Ruff and Scrappy after us by now, we were hoping to just get the money back to Chestnut so he could deal with it."

Ana sighed. Blanche and Buck turned to look at her. Buck started to chortle. "Ah HA! I *knew* it. There it is."

"There's what?" asked Ana, cautiously.

"The *real* reason you went after those drugs," said Blanche. "I'd recognize it anywhere."

"It's the thrill of giving in to the dark side," said Buck in a low voice with a big grin.

"Like in *Star Wars?*" Artie asked.

"Sorta," said Buck. "Only this is real life. And nothing makes you feel more alive than the thought that you might not be soon. Am I right?"

It was quiet for a moment. Emily stared down at the plate of food and thought about this. Was that really the reason she was in this mess? Just the sheer excitement? The pull of doing something she'd never do otherwise? Is that why she'd suddenly felt compelled to *prove* that she wasn't an uptight perfectionist?

"YOLO," said Brandon, softly. "That's why we're in this mess."

"What?" Blanche asked, her mug inches from her mouth.

"YOLO," Brandon said again. "It's an acronym for You Only Live Once."

"You're damned right, son," said Buck. "And if you want to stay alive—"

"And outta prison—" Blanche broke in.

"You gotta be smart about it," said Buck. "Which, lucky for you, Stanley is not."

"I don't think he has to be very smart to send Ruff and Scrappy after us," said Emily.

Buck shook his head. "And do what? Stanley's not a killer.

Neither are these goons he's got working for him. Last I heard he was trying to hire minor-league baseball players to work as his muscle."

"He sure looked like a killer to me," said Brandon.

"Got that scar tripping down some stairs into a plate-glass window," said Blanche. "Only thing he's ever killed was his own prospects."

Emily was suddenly struck with an idea that would allow them to ditch the money and head straight for the party. "Do you think you could give the money to Chestnut and Liz when they come back for Artie?" she asked.

"Absolutely not." Buck threw up both hands like she'd pulled a gun on him.

"We'd never hear the end of that," Blanche sighed. "The last time we tried to get involved in one of his deals, Liz had a meltdown and blamed us when the whole thing went wrong."

"Threatened to keep us from seeing Artie," said Buck. "That's a deal breaker for us."

Emily smiled. Maybe they had been bad guys once upon a time, and perhaps their parenting skills weren't so spectacular, but Blanche and Buck sure seemed to have their priorities squared away now. "Can I ask you a question?"

"Shoot," said Blanche.

"Why'd you two stop? I mean, even with all the technology and cameras in banks now, there must've been *something* you could've kept doing."

"That's the first rule of living outside the system," said Buck. "Get out while you're ahead."

"We have what we need." Blanche motioned around her kitchen. "At a certain point, you can't spend any more money. Besides, every time you set out on a heist, it's a gamble." She reached over and ran her hand through Artie's head. "And some things are just too precious to take a chance on."

"So what do we do with this suitcase of cash?" Brandon asked.

Buck stroked his beard and thought for a second. "I guess if you really want to give it Chestnut, you could head over to Frank's."

"Who's Frank?" asked Ana.

"Frank's not a person," said Buck. "It's a pool hall."

Blanche explained that it was Liz's favorite hangout. "She and Chestnut met there."

"I thought they met in high school," said Ana.

"That's correct," said Blanche. "They spent most of high school cutting class and hustling pool. Chestnut won a date with Liz by beating her two outta three."

"Think they'll be there now?" Emily asked.

"Worth a shot," said Buck. "That's usually where they land after their deals get screwed up." He winked at Emily. "And I think this certainly qualifies in that department."

Buck and Blanche walked them out to the car, and Artie gave each of them a hug good-bye and kissed Pickles on the head.

"Thanks for the coffee and food," said Emily.

"And the advice," said Brandon.

"Thanks for bringing our boy back," said Blanche. "I may just brain his father next time I see him."

"Should we send them your way if we see them at Frank's?" Emily asked.

"Hell no," roared Buck from the porch with a feisty smile.

As she pulled out of the driveway, Emily saw Buck reach over and slide his arm around Blanche's waist. He pulled her close and gave her a big kiss. She melted into him and kicked a high heel up behind her like they were on a TV show. Artie was waving as they slipped out of sight, and Emily realized that Blanche and Buck loved each other just the way they were—no changes necessary. It was probably the secret to their success.

Suddenly it was like a light bulb had gone off in her head. Buck and Blanche were happy because they had their own values, and they followed them. They didn't change for anybody, and while they'd gotten where they are through questionable means, they didn't become different people while doing it. That's what made them happy.

Emily knew she just wanted to be happy, with her life and her relationships . . . and maybe that meant staying true to herself and not changing for anyone. Even someone like Kyle.

But the first step to making her life right and getting back on track was to get to that party.

chapter 20

As Emily pulled into the parking lot of Frank's Billiard Hall, Brandon was still trying to convince her not to stop.

"This is our worst idea yet," he said. "We don't even know if they'll be here, so we're just gonna hang out at a pool hall in a strip mall . . . until what? They close?"

Emily put the car in park and turned off the engine. "Look," she said, "I still want to get to that party, and this makes some sense as a plan. We're out of the way of danger, but might still be able to get things back on track."

"Anyway, Buck and Blanche suggested it," Ana said. "And they would know, right?" She snuggled Pickles, who barked his agreement.

"We don't have all night," Brandon whined.

"We can't go back to the warehouse," Emily said. "Big Dog would know by now that we're not the right people, and he might not be dangerous, but I don't want to risk it."

"And it would take way too long to get back there," Ana pointed out. "And maybe for nothing. Liz and Chestnut will probably show up here, just like Blanche and Buck said. We can wait until, I don't know, seven, and if they're not here, we'll head out then. We'll still make it to the Steins' with enough time to shower, change, and get ready."

Brandon signed loudly. "I don't know why I ever agreed to go with you guys. I should've known it'd turn into something. It *always* turns into something with the two of you. Instead, I could've slept in, then headed up with some of the guys. We would've played some pool, some X-Box, chilled, partied, whatever. There would be no diner heist, no cocaine, no suitcases of money, no children, and no Chihuahuas."

Pickles barked his annoyance.

"Well, it's too late to turn back now, Brandon," Ana said. "And anyway . . . YOLO, right?"

Brandon looked like he was about to explode, but finally he rubbed his eyes and nodded. "Yeah. YOLO."

"If they don't show up in an hour, we'll just keep the money," Ana said. "We tried our best. No harm, no foul. We never even told anyone our names . . . I don't think."

Emily thought back, trying to remember how specific they'd gotten at any moment, but she wasn't really sure. And she wasn't sure it even mattered. It sounded like Buck and Blanche weren't all too concerned about their son and daughter-in-law, who also didn't sound like the kind of people to track someone down. Big Dog definitely didn't know who to look for. The only hope would be that Big Dog wouldn't go after Artie again, but if Buck and Blanche weren't concerned . . .

"Let's just hope they're here," Emily said, shaking her

head. "Maybe they'll talk to Buck and Blanche and come here to find us."

"Fine." Brandon opened the car door. "But I'd just like to reserve the right to say 'I told you so' if this whole thing goes south."

"Duly noted," said Emily.

Ana was touching up her eyeliner in the mirror on the passenger-side visor. "I don't think you'll have time for that," she said.

"What do you mean?" Brandon asked.

"I mean if the dealers come for you, you won't have time to say 'I told you so.'"

"Thanks for that. Really appreciate the vote of confidence." He jumped out of the car and slammed the door, then stalked into Frank's.

Emily joined Ana for a moment touching up her lipstick and dabbing a little powder onto her forehead and nose. "He's so uptight about this," she said.

Ana started laughing. "Look who's talking, *mamacita*."

Emily smiled. "I've turned over a new leaf. Sort of."

Ana blotted her fresh lipstick on a tissue and turned to Emily. "How do I look? Damage control?"

"You're good," said Emily. Then she stopped and turned back, staring at her friend. "Oh. My. God."

"What?" said Ana.

"You're totally going to flirt with Brandon right now, aren't you?"

"What? No! I just . . . wanted to—" Ana sputtered and stuttered until Emily shook her head slowly and held up a hand.

"It's fine," she said. "You two have actually been really cute today."

"*Loca*," Ana muttered under her breath as she shoved her makeup back into her purse. "I have no idea what you're talking about." She jumped out of the car and headed into the pool hall.

Emily smiled and locked the car, then followed Ana inside. It took a second for her eyes to adjust. The cigarette smoke was thick and hung heavy in the air, and she realized it was a good thing that they'd all come in at different times. Every guy in the place was staring at Ana's ass as she wiggled in at the bar next to Brandon, who had already ordered and was waiting for his drink, so Emily was able to slip in without being seen.

She walked down the side of the pool hall opposite the bar. The pool tables were lined up the length of the right side of the place, and the bar ran down the left side. After she made a lap around the pool tables without seeing Liz or Chestnut, she joined Brandon and Ana at the bar.

Brandon was swigging a Budweiser. "Did you see them?" he asked.

"Nope," said Emily. "Did they check your ID?"

Brandon cocked his head with a smirk. "Cheers," he said, holding up his beer bottle and taking a big gulp.

Ana turned around from the bar, holding a Cosmo. "So, what's the plan now?" she asked.

"This is no fair!" Emily said. "Why do I always have to be the one who drives?"

"Oh, you can have just one," said Ana.

"No. No, I cannot," said Emily. "And the plan is that we wait right here and watch the door until seven. Then we are going to the party."

Brandon surveyed the pool tables around the room. "I dunno, Em. Looks like we may already be at the party."

"No, *Brans*, we are not."

"You know what would be fun?" said Brandon with a sly grin. "Playing a little pool while we wait."

"Yes!" Ana jumped off the barstool.

Emily sighed. "Fine. Go for it. I'm going to get a Coke and sit right here to watch the door. Check in with you in fifteen minutes?"

"Deal," Brandon said.

"Have a *real* drink," Ana said. "It'll help you lighten up."

"No dice," said Emily. "Fifteen minutes. Come back and check in."

"Fine," said Ana.

"You ready for me to take you to Pool School?" Brandon asked her.

"You're not taking me *anywhere*, white boy." Ana's eyes flashed a challenge.

"Care to make it interesting?" Brandon asked.

"Bring it," said Ana. She spun on her heel, flipped her hair, and turned every head in the room as she walked from the bar to an empty pool table.

"Sounds like you're the commander in chief."

Emily turned to the guy sitting on the barstool to her right and suddenly couldn't make her mouth work to talk. The guy's dark hair was cropped close on the sides and longish on top, but not fussy, sort of swept up and messy. His complexion was tanned, like he spent time outside but not at the tanning salon. His eyes were dark, too, and held the spark of a joke—only she'd forgotten what he said now.

"Excuse me?" she asked, a nervous smile tugging at the corners of her mouth.

"Just sounds like you're calling the shots with those two," he said. Then he smiled, and Emily thought she might fall of her stool. His smile was a little crooked, his jaw chiseled out of stone, and there was a little dent in his chin that she couldn't stop staring at. She kept imagining running her tongue over it.

Pull it together, she told herself. *He's* talking *to you.*

She laughed a little and tried to marshal the power of speech. "Yeah," she said. "I guess I am."

"You don't sound too enthused about being in charge," he said. Something about the way he said it surprised Emily. It wasn't like he was just making small talk with somebody he'd met thirty seconds ago. He actually seemed to care how she felt about this.

Emily shrugged. "Yeah, it's . . . been a hard day."

He polished off a beer. "I get it," he said. "What are you drinking?"

"Nothing yet," she said. "Diet Coke?"

He nodded, and Emily was relieved when he didn't give her a hard time, just waved down the bartender and got her a soda.

"Thanks," she said.

"You're welcome. I'm Chris, by the way."

"Emily." She squeezed the lime into her Diet and took a sip from the straw.

"So, how'd you get saddled with the being in charge?"

"We're on our way to a party," she explained. "A whole weekend, really. Just drove up today. I guess we just sort of fall into these roles." Emily braced herself. This is where the cute guy who barely knew her told her to lighten up and have some fun, to let go and live a little.

Instead, Chris just nodded. "It suits you."

An involuntary look of surprise crossed her face. "Really?"

"Don't people tell you that?" he asked.

Emily laughed. "Never. All I hear is how I'm too uptight and need to loosen up."

Chris shook his head. "I disagree."

"You don't really know me, though," Emily said.

Chris shrugged. "True. But I know me. And I like a woman who knows what she wants and doesn't need someone else's approval to get it."

When he said those words, Emily had the sensation that a something had broken free inside of her. She smiled at Chris. "That might be the nicest thing a guy has said to me in a long time."

Chris smiled back. "That just tells me that you've been hanging out with the wrong guys."

Emily laughed. "And what about now?"

Chris raised his bottle of Heineken. "Now you're hanging out with the right ones."

chapter 21

After Chris ordered another beer, Emily told him she needed to check in with her friends.

"Need company?"

"They're just right there," Emily said, pointing.

"I know. I just don't think you should go by yourself."

"Because . . . it's . . . dangerous?" she asked. They might've been in a pool hall, but none of the people seemed particularly deadly. Especially considering the rest of her day.

"No." Chris looked her straight in the eyes. "Because I'll miss you."

This answer delighted Emily, but she tried not to smile because she didn't want to appear to be *too* delighted. She didn't even know this guy. No matter how nice he seemed, he was just a momentary acquaintance. "Is that what you tell all the girls?" she asked, trying to keep her voice steady.

Chris looked over both shoulders, scanning the room, then turned back to her. "You're the only woman under thirty-five in this place. I don't tell the rest of these people anything."

Emily laughed. "Fine. Come with me."

They found Brandon beating the pants off a guy at what was apparently a low-stakes table in the corner.

"What does low-stakes mean?" Emily asked.

"They've only got twenty dollars riding on this game," Ana explained.

"Wait, they're *betting* on this game?" Emily couldn't believe it. "I mean, Brandon is trying to make money?"

"Oh, he's not *trying*," said Ana. "He's succeeding. He's up to forty already. This will be sixty."

As she said that, Emily watched as Brandon sunk the last two balls on the table with a behind-the-back shot that looked like a move that only worked in a movie. Ana jumped up and down and ran over and hugged him.

"We're not supposed to think they're . . . together?" Chris asked Emily.

Emily shrugged. "It's a developing thing."

"Sounds like there's a story."

She looked at Chris. "Isn't there always?" She motioned to her friends. "In their case, they're both friends of mine who started dating, and then crashed and burned. Things seem to be rekindling today, though."

"And how do you feel about that?"

"I wasn't for it at first," Emily admitted. "But now . . . I wonder if maybe the time apart has given them some perspective. Maybe they'd actually be good together, you know?"

"Well, if they're both friends with you, they've got to have great taste."

Emily turned to Chris again and allowed herself to give him a smile this time.

"You know, you should get your friend to play that table." Chris pointed to another corner. "He's good. *Really* good, considering the types that hang out around here."

After Emily had introduced Chris and Brandon, Chris explained the high-stakes table and, without much effort, convinced Brandon to give it a shot. The buy-in was five hundred and Brandon was about to bow out, saying he didn't have that much cash on him, when Ana pulled a wad of bills out of her pocket. Emily and Brandon both stared at her in shock, but she just shrugged.

Brandon's first game went by quickly. His opponent seemed to be loaded, but completely without skill. The second game was against the same player, so in no time at all, Brandon was up a thousand dollars and a crowd had formed around the table to see the new guy, and people had lined up to play him.

"So how'd your friend get this good?" Chris asked.

"His dad," Emily said. "I think they used to play when he was younger. I had no idea he was this good, though."

"Everyone's full of surprises," Chris muttered.

Emily glanced at him out of the corner of her eye, wondering what sorts of surprises he might have. Not that she cared. It wouldn't be long before they parted ways forever.

It wasn't long before Brandon had cleared twenty-five hundred. It seemed like people in this town weren't hurting for cash—farming was apparently more lucrative than Emily could've imagined—and everyone seemed more enamored by Brandon's skill than hurt by their losses. A few of the female patrons were enamored enough to try to slip in next to Brandon to give him a good-luck kiss before shots, but Ana was pretty quick to shut down each and every one of the women, and Brandon didn't seem to mind one bit.

Everything seemed to be going pretty smoothly until there was some commotion on the other side of the pool hall. Emily didn't think anything of it at first, and Chris said that someone was probably just stumbling from one too many beers, but when Emily glanced at Ana and saw her friend's wide-eyed stare, she quickly turned to look.

Big Dog, along with his henchmen Ruff and Scrappy, was standing by the door, looking around. Looking for *them*.

Emily immediately ducked behind Chris, and then behind the pool table. She quickly crouch-waddled her way to Ana and pulled the girl down behind her.

"They found us," Ana hissed. "We're *so* dead."

"How'd they even know we were here?" Emily wasn't sure why she was asking Ana this. Neither of them would know the answer. It barely made any sense . . . but most of the day made little sense, so they should've assumed his would happen.

"Hey there." Chris was suddenly crouched next to them, grinning. "Someone loose a contact lens? Or maybe an earring?"

"This is *so* much worse, *mano*," Ana said, shaking her head

Emily put her hand back over Ana's mouth. "Shh!" She

turned to Chris, keeping her hand in place on Ana's mouth. "There's no way to explain all of this, but some guys are looking for us."

"Like ex-boyfriends?" Chris asked.

"Like drug dealers we ripped off." Emily couldn't believe she'd just said this out loud, but there was no other choice. She felt her heart sink. She wouldn't be getting Chris's number, that much was certain.

Chris frowned. "Wait. You mean *Stanley?*"

"Does *everyone* know this guy?" Emily asked.

"Hang on." Chris stood up again, slipping into the crowd of people who were cheering Brandon on. Brandon still hadn't realized that anything strange was going on, and all of his focus was centered on the pool table and his rapidly thickening wallet.

Chris returned a moment later and said, "They're making their way down the bar, asking around. I don't think they've seen you yet."

"They think Brandon's name is Chestnut," said Emily. "And they think I'm a girl named Liz."

"I really want to know why, but let's discuss at a later time, shall we?" Chris reached over and grabbed a pool cue off the wall. With one well-aimed move he waved it under the table and smacked Brandon in the shin on the other side. Brandon yelped "Ow!" and was immediately on all fours, his head appearing under the table.

"Hey!" he said, frowning at Emily, Chris, and Ana. "I was

wondering where you guys went. Did you hit me?" People started attempting to pull Brandon up so he could take his next shot. "Hang on! Hang on a minute!" he shouted up at them. He looked back at Emily. "I have to go."

"BIG DOG." Emily hissed under the table, pointing toward the bar.

Brandon's eyes went wide. "*Shit*." He crawled on all fours under the table to where they were. "What do we do?"

Chris jabbed a thumb behind him. "There's a back door by the bathrooms. Let's make a break on 'three,' okay?"

Everybody nodded. Chris counted. They stood up.

Emily realized immediately that they should have either (a) stayed down and crawled to the bathroom, or (b) spaced out, standing up one at a time. As it was, they'd all popped up like a barbershop quartet, immediately turning every head toward them, including Scrappy, who was three tables over. For the first time ever, they heard Scrappy speak:

"HEY!"

Big Dog and Ruff spun around from their search at the bar, and Ruff leaped into action, immediately jumping chairs and pool tables to get to them.

"Get them!" Big Dog shouted.

Chris grabbed Emily's hand and started pulling her toward the bathroom, leaving Emily just a second to grab Ana, who was already holding on to Brandon. The four of them stumbled and shoved their way to the back of the pool hall and were quickly engulfed by the large crowd that had accumulated to watch Brandon's billiard game, which kept Ruff and Big Dog at bay.

"Go! Go! Go!" Brandon shouted as they plowed through the lines at the bathrooms and the pool hall turned into an arena, with fights breaking out in every corner because of the pushing and shoving that was happening.

At the back doors Emily looked back to see that Ruff and Scrappy were both involved in pretty big fights, which they seemed to be losing, and Big Dog was being held down on a pool table as he kicked and screamed to be released immediately. She couldn't help but let out a laugh of joy when she saw the perfect scene before her.

"Come on, troublemaker," Chris said as he slipped an arm around her waist and pulled her toward the doorway. "You can laugh at the brawl you caused when we're safely away from your drug-dealer pursuers."

Outside, the four raced around the corner of the building and came out in the front parking lot where Emily's SUV was waiting for them in front of Frank's, thankfully intact and untouched. The car lights flashed when Emily hit the button on her keychain, and Brandon dove into the backseat, causing a barking fit from Pickles, who was either happy to see them or angry about being woken up.

"Come on, Em!" Ana shouted as she jumped into the passenger side and hit the side of the car. "We've got to get out of here."

On the driver's side, Emily stopped and turned to Chris,

who was standing next to her with his hands shoved into his jeans pockets and a small smirk.

He raised an eyebrow and cocked his head toward the pool hall. "So . . . that was fun," he said. "Didn't expect that kind of excitement when I woke up this morning."

"Me neither," Emily said, shaking her head. "I'm so sorry I got you involved."

"Don't be," he said quickly. "It was nice. Things can get pretty dull around here. Monotonous. You guys livened things up."

Emily hesitated, not sure what to do or say next. She knew they had to go—Brandon's moans and mumbling from the backseat made that abundantly clear—but she felt like she and Chris had some kind of connection. Maybe it was because he'd just saved her from some drug dealers . . . but maybe it was something more than that. And she felt like she wanted to explore the possibility of . . . what? There wasn't any possibility. She didn't know him, he didn't know her, and this was just a momentary hiccup in the day's plan. Nothing more.

"So I've gotta go," she said, regretting the words even as they left her mouth.

"You should," Chris said, nodding.

The pause that happened was on the sort of epic scale that Emily thought could only happen in romantic comedies and on daytime soaps she used to catch bits of when she stayed home sick. It was like everything around them, everything other than Chris, ceased to exist, and there was nothing she wanted more than to just jump into his arms, press her body against his, and make their lips touch and never stop touching.

"I'll find you," he whispered, just loud enough for her to hear.

"How?"

"I have my ways."

"But . . ."

"A girl like you doesn't come along every day," Chris said. "And now that I've found one, I'm not going to let her get away that easily. Stanley be damned."

"Come *onnnnnn, chica!*" Ana shouted. "*Vámonos!*"

Chris reached behind Emily and pulled the door open. "Trust me," he said as he gently pushed her into the car.

Emily wasn't sure how or why, but she knew that she did trust him. Without another word, she closed the door, started the car, and pulled out of the parking lot. In her rearview mirror, Chris became smaller and smaller until she turned the corner and couldn't see him anymore. But she knew, or hoped at least, that it wouldn't be the last time.

chapter 22

"Earth to Emily!" Ana called out. "Come in, Emily."

"Huh? What?" Emily refocused and glanced at her friend in the passenger seat. "What is it? I'm fine. I'm paying attention." She looked ahead to be sure, but her driving was on point, as usual.

"I'm not worried about your driving," Ana said. "You're a perfect driver, and you know it. Even when your head is in the clouds and your heart is about to explode."

"I don't know what you're talking about." Her heart *was* racing, though. But that might've had to do with the fact that they'd just dodged a potentially major bar fight.

"Come on, *dime todo*," Ana said. "Tell me everything!"

"Everything about *what*?" Emily knew exactly what Ana was talking about, but she refused to make it easy for her. If she wanted information, she was going to work for it.

"Pah-*leeze*," Brandon said. "Even I could see the tension there, and I'm emotionally and romantically stunted, according to Ana."

"It was *nothing*," Emily said.

"Looked like something to me," Ana shot back. "But he was cute, so I totally approve. Maybe a little on the older side, but I think you need that kind of maturity. You're much too sophisticated for high-school boys."

"When did you become the queen of relationships?" Emily asked.

"Girl, I've learned from my mistakes."

"*Ouch!*" Brandon said loudly. "Harsh."

"All I'm saying," Ana continued, "is that he seemed like a good guy, and you should get to know him a little more. Invite him to the party."

"I'll second that," Brandon said. "I liked the dude."

"Well . . . you see . . ." Emily let out a sigh. "I don't have his number."

"What?!"

Ana's screech sent Pickles into a barking frenzy, and Emily had to actually concentrate to get the car back on track after an unintentional swerve.

"Please don't do that again," Emily said.

"Please don't forget to ask for a cute guy's phone number!" Ana shouted.

"We never really had a chance to talk about it," Emily said. "I didn't really expect Big Dog to show up right then."

Ana sighed and collapsed in her seat. "Just when I thought you'd made some progress . . ." Ana sat up quickly and looked in the side mirror. "What's going on behind us?"

Emily checked out her rearview and frowned at the car flashing its lights behind them. "Is something wrong with the car? Are they telling us to pull over?"

"Dude, that car is moving pretty fast," Brandon said. "It's gaining on us . . . do you think?"

"It can't be." Ana shook her head. "Could it?"

"Can't what?"

"Is it Big Dog?" Brandon turned forward. "We *have* to call the police." He pulled his phone out, but Ana snatched it from him a second later. "Hey!"

"We're not calling anyone."

"Give me my phone, Ana! I'm calling."

"We don't even know who it is," Ana argued. "And if it is Big Dog, what's calling the police going to do now? We won't have the money, *and* we'll probably get arrested."

"If we're not calling the police, then we have to outrun them," Brandon said. "Emily, you've got to forget all of those driving rules and *put the pedal to the metal*."

Emily would've laughed at Brandon's clichéd phrase, but the situation wasn't particularly funny, so she just did as she was told. Her hands gripped the wheel and immediately started to sweat, though she wasn't sure if it was because of the speed or because the car was still gaining on them.

"Go faster!" Brandon shouted.

"I can only go so fast!" Emily shouted back. She was going as fast as she dared to, but it still didn't seem to be enough. But she didn't want to push it and end up killing all of them. They were starting to reach the mountains now—not too far from the Steins'—and the curves on the highway were made more complicated and dangerous because of the wind and trees . . . not to mention the potential for deer.

"These assholes are crazy!" Brandon said as the car came up on their left side.

As the car pulled into view, Emily saw why: Liz was leaning out the passenger window screaming at the top of her lungs while Chestnut honked and flashed the lights, cursing and swerving all over the place.

"PULL OVER!" Liz was cursing a blue streak and waving her arms. The look in her eyes chilled Emily to the bone.

"What do I do?!" she screamed.

"Hit the brakes!" Brandon shouted.

"What?!" Ana interrupted her pretty-much-nonstop screaming to ask.

"But—"

"They'll surge ahead and we'll be able to get away," Brandon said. "I've seen it in a million movies. Do it!"

Emily wasn't sure they should be taking driving tips from action movies, especially since cinematic life advice hadn't worked particularly well for them the rest of the day, but she barely even got a chance to consider the option before Chestnut jerked his car to the side, crashing right into the SUV.

Emily felt the car begin to skid, and she gripped the steering wheel as the right back wheel caught the edge of the pavement and they spun onto the shoulder of the road. The momentum carried the passenger side of the car up into the air, and Emily heard Brandon yell, "Oh shit!" It felt like they might keep rolling all the way over, but they skidded for a few yards on two wheels and then the passenger side slammed back down to the ground, causing the air bags in front of Emily and Ana to explode out of the steering wheel and dash as they skidded to a stop, the whole car rocking back and forth.

Before Emily could even take a breath, Liz was banging on the hood. Chestnut was right behind her.

"Where is he? Where is Artie?" Liz was spitting and screaming and smacking at the door and window.

Emily and Ana struggled against their seat belts and the air bags as Brandon kicked open the back door. Almost immediately he was being pulled out and dragged across the ground by Chestnut and Liz. Emily tried to push open her door, but when she found that it was too jammed, she crawled into the backseat and jumped out of the car that way.

"Stop! Stop!" she screamed as she ran to the fight in front of her. She grabbed Liz and tried to pull her away, and was soon joined by Ana and Pickles, who went straight for Chestnut's ankles. "Stop!"

"You stole the money!" Chestnut shouted as he stumbled away from Pickles.

"You kidnapped my baby!" Liz screamed as she raced to the car, calling Artie's name. "Where is he?"

"Everybody, *shut up!*" Ana shouted so loud that everyone went silent, staring at her with surprise. Even Pickles stopped his yapping to stare.

Emily turned to Liz. "Artie is completely fine, no thanks to you."

"What's that supposed to mean?" Liz asked, frowning.

Emily couldn't believe it. "You've got to be kidding me. You left him with some mobsters at a pizza place so you could go do some small shop hits before heading over to pick up some drugs. What about that says good parenting?"

"You don't know the situation," Chestnut said as he started to explain.

"And I don't care," Emily interrupted. "You'd better be happy you have a good, smart boy, and parents that are willing and able to take care of him."

"He'd be better off without you two," Brandon put in, his voice shaking with anger.

Emily looked at her friend and saw that Brandon's face was bright red and his fists were clenched at his sides, like it was taking everything in him not to jump at Chestnut and tackle him to the ground. Emily wondered if Brandon's anger was coming from his own experience with a father who wasn't a particularly good parent. She had issues with her own dad, that was for sure, but that was nothing compared to what Brandon had gone through, and the way Artie was being raised wasn't much better.

"If you want to do the right thing," Emily said, turning her attention to the thieving couple again, "then you'll get out of the business, just like Buck and Blanche have."

"You met my parents?" Chestnut seemed confused.

"We did, and if you don't get your acts together I might just go back to their house and tell them to keep Artie forever," Ana put in.

"We didn't mean for it to happen his way," Liz said. "We don't ever want to put Artie in danger. We love that boy."

"Then show it," Brandon said. "Get out of the business, because you don't know what you're doing and you never will, and you're just condemning him to a horrible life, whether that means you two get caught, or worse, Artie gets hurt because of your idiocy."

"This was supposed to be the last job," Liz said. "The last job like this. That's why we're here. Normally we wouldn't have cared, especially for someone like Big Dog, but we're trying to build up a little bit of money so Chestnut here can go back to school."

"Gotta finish my business degree," Chestnut said proudly. "Accounting."

Emily narrowed her eyes and looked at Ana and Brandon, who seemed just as confused. "You're in school?"

"Just two more classes left," Chestnut said. "And then I can get a real job. My parents don't know."

"We've been keeping it a secret, so we could surprise them," Liz explained. "Artie starts school this fall, and we wanted to make sure he could be proud of us around his friends and classmates. When Chestnut's got a real job, then maybe I can open up the cake shop I've dreamed about since I was a little girl."

Emily felt like the world had been turned completely on its head. "You want a *cake shop?*"

"Well, we'd have other pastries too, of course," Liz said slowly, like the *cake* was the part Emily was questioning.

Emily let out a slow breath of air. "Artie is fine," she said again. "And the money is in the trunk. Brandon?"

Brandon was still fuming, but it looked like he'd calmed down a little after hearing Chestnut and Liz's ultimate plans. He crawled into the car and came out a moment later, suitcase in tow. He carried it over to the group and handed it to Chestnut, who nodded solemnly.

"Sorry about . . ." Liz motioned at the car. "That wasn't really planned."

Emily stared at her car, really seeing the damage for the first time. It was completely totaled, or close to it. She was surprised, shocked even, that they'd made it out completely fine. The front was crushed, and it looked like her and Ana's doors had somehow fused with the rest of the frame. The back of the car seemed okay . . . save for the fact that both back wheels were completely missing. She glanced around and saw that they'd left them a couple yards back.

"Do you need a ride?" Chestnut asked. "We could take you to a gas station."

"Uh . . ." Emily had no idea what she needed anymore.

"We'll be fine," Brandon said, shaking his head. "We'll just call a tow truck. I'm sure they'll be here in no time at all."

"You sure?" Liz asked. "I feel terrible."

"We're fine," Brandon said. "Really. Just go get Artie, and pull yourselves together. For him."

Chestnut and Liz nodded, and Emily was surprised that she actually felt a little pang of emotion as they made their way to their car, turned it around, then sped down the road.

"Well . . . ," Ana said with a sigh. "At least they have a game plan." She looked at Brandon. "Why didn't you want their help?"

"We are *finally* free of all of the craziness that's happened today," Brandon said. "We made it through a diner holdup, a convenience store holdup, a drug pickup, a drop-off, a child, a pool hall brawl, and a car crash. We're *so* close to the Steins', I can taste the Jose Cuervo. I don't want to mess it up by riding with Chestnut and Liz. We'll just call for a tow truck and, in the meantime, have someone come down from the house to get us. Easy."

"Only one problem," Emily said as she stared at her phone screen. "I don't have any bars."

chapter 23

Brandon pulled out his phone and his shoulders fell. "Well, I didn't see this coming. . . ."

"It's because we're so close to the mountains," Emily said, glancing their way. "Reception is going to be spotty."

"Or nonexistent," Ana said as she peered over Emily's shoulder. "Looks like we should've taken that offer for a ride." She looked pointedly at Brandon.

Brandon was still cursing under his breath as he climbed up on top of Emily's car and held his cell over his head. Finally, he joined Emily and Ana who had crawled back into the car to wait, and reclined their seats a little. As Brandon slid into the backseat, Emily started to laugh. She couldn't help it. As she thought of all of the ways that she had planned for this day to go, this ending had never even been a remote possibility.

Ana sat up and looked at her. "You're freaking me out. Why are you laughing?"

Emily finally got ahold of herself for long enough to speak. "Because this has to be the single most ridiculous day in the history of the world," she said, wiping tears from her eyes. "I mean, if I'd sat down and tried to *make up* a bad day, I wouldn't have been able to come up with this shit in a billion years."

"Truth *is* stranger than fiction," Brandon said.

"So, how much money did we actually leave the pool hall with?" Ana asked as she turned in her seat.

Brandon pulled the wad of bills out of his pocket and counted out $2728, most of it in singles, fives, and twenties. "Not a bad haul for us today," he said.

"Us?" said Emily. "You earned it. That's your money."

"Nah," said Brandon. "This whole day has been a team effort."

"Yeah." Ana laughed. "It takes more than one idiot to mess up a road trip this badly."

All three of them cracked up at this point, and Emily felt all of the tension and frustration of the past eight hours slip away.

"Oh my God," she said as the realization set in, "has it only been *eight hours* since we got on the highway?"

"Jesus," said Brandon. "It feels like it's been eight *days*."

"We managed to pack a lot of living into this day." Emily smiled.

"YOLO, bitches," said Ana. "YOLO."

"So," Brandon said as he leaned forward. "What's the plan?"

"I don't know," said Ana. "But we need to come up with something quick." She rubbed her hand up and down on Pickle's tummy. "This poor little guy hasn't had anything to eat for a while. And the last time he had water was at Buck and Blanche's place. So, what do we do?"

Emily could only shrug. "I've got nothin'. I guess we just wait for somebody to drive by and try to flag them down."

"Are you crazy?" said Ana. "What if it's some backwoods serial killer?"

Emily laughed. "Oh, c'mon. After our day?"

"After our day, that's even more likely," Ana pointed out.

"I guess I'll have to walk to get some help," said Brandon.

"Don't even try it." Ana was having none of it. "That's just asking to be kidnapped and killed."

"So the options are that we're picked up by a highway killer," Brandon said, "or I get kidnapped and killed while walking along the side of the road. How is the first option any better?"

"At least then we'll be together."

Despite how morbid Ana's conclusion was, Emily couldn't help but smile at the comment. Leave it to Ana to somehow turn the potential moment of death into an opportunity for strengthened friendship.

"Hey, Emily, can you pop the hood?" Brandon asked.

"You're not going to be able to fix the car," Ana said.

"Obviously. But that way if someone drives by, they'll know we're having car trouble."

"I think it's pretty obvious," Emily said as she tried to pop the hood, but no matter how many times she pulled the level, the hood didn't move. "Looks like that's not happening." She sighed and sat back in her seat.

The sun had slipped behind the mountains and the sky had turned a lovely shade of indigo. Through the cracked windshield, Emily could see stars twinkling to life. As the sky grew darker, there were other lights in the sky, too, including three bright, red-carpet style beams that broke through the trees and lit up the sky. Emily knew they had to be coming from the Steins'. Jacob knew how to throw a party, and the setup was always fantastic, from music to drinks to food. There was always something for everyone.

"This sucks," Ana mumbled.

"Major," Brandon added.

Emily was about to suggest walking up the hill to the Steins', when two more lights appeared, this time coming toward them up the highway. Brandon was out of the car in a second and in the middle of the road, jumping and screaming while waving his arms in the air.

"Does he really think they're not going to see him?" Ana asked. "It's not like he's hidden."

"He's just trying to help," Emily said.

"I know." Emily could hear Ana's smile as she said it.

As the car got closer, Emily could see that it was a silver sedan. Even when the car started to slow down, Brandon continued to shout and jump like he was flagging down an entire fleet of planes. Emily was impressed by his dedication to saving them, but she couldn't keep out of her mind the possibility that Big Dog had found them. And no matter how many people laughed at his antics and called him Stanley, she couldn't get out of her head that he was a real, legit, drug dealer. That still counted for something.

"Well, look at this."

Emily stared out the window, not believing her eyes. Brandon had stopped jumping and was also staring, though probably for a different reason.

"*Dios mio,*" Ana said. "Talk about fate."

There, in the car that had just pulled up to rescue them, was Chris.

chapter 24

Emily felt like she would melt when Chris threw an arm over her shoulder as he surveyed the damage to her car.

"And all of you are okay?"

"Amazingly," Ana said.

"And you didn't get their insurance information?"

"They were career criminals," Brandon said. "Do you really think they have insurance?"

"Good point." Chris nodded slowly, then pulled Emily closer. "I'm just glad none of you were hurt."

"What about cell service?" Ana asked. "So we can get a tow truck out here?"

"Not in this part of the mountains," Chris said, shaking his head. "Once you get up higher, there are satellites to help out, but where we are now . . . nothing."

"You know," Ana said slowly, like she'd just come up with a brilliant idea, "we could just go to the party. You could come with us, Chris."

"I wasn't sure if it was some kind of private affair," Chris said.

"Oh please," Ana said. "Jacob and Madison don't know the meaning of *private*."

"Madison sure doesn't," Brandon said, earning a stern glare from Ana.

"Well . . . if that's okay."

Emily didn't catch on until Ana stomped her foot.

"Oh, right, yeah, definitely," she said quickly, turning to Chris and trying to get her bearings. "Please come. Yeah."

Chris smiled and shook his head. "What about your car?"

"We can call someone when we get to the Steins'," Ana said as she hustled to the destroyed car and climbed into the backseat so she could start pulling things from the trunk. "Okay, if we go now I should still have enough time to shower and change and get my makeup on." She reappeared holding a suitcase.

"I thought you gave the money back," Chris said slowly. "Please don't tell me it was one of those hoaxes where you gave them an empty suitcase and now you've got the cash and you're going to try to get away with it."

"This is my party gear," Ana said with a frown, as if that should've been completely obvious. "How would I get ready without my party gear?"

Chris narrowed his eyes and looked at Emily. "And yours?"

Ana held up a small backpack. "And it's not even full. I don't know how she does it."

Emily rolled her eyes as she took the bag, then motioned for everyone to head to Chris's car. Chris and Brandon went quickly, but Ana held Emily back.

"So how amazing is this?" she hissed. "It's totally fate."

Emily had to admit that things were finally starting to come together. Chris's reappearance was almost like the universe was apologizing for the day it'd put her through. And she definitely accepted that apology.

Once in the car, with Emily in the front seat, and Brandon, Ana, and Pickles in the back, Chris said, "When we're higher up on the mountain, I'll give the police a call."

"Is that going to be a problem?" Emily asked. "Getting the police involved, I mean."

"Nah, it's my Uncle Bud," Chris said. "It'll be fine. He'll do me a favor."

"Wait, Bud as in Sheriff Bud?" Brandon asked. "Dude . . ."

"We were pulled over by your uncle earlier today." Emily relayed the whole story to Chris. "That's seriously your uncle?"

"Yeah, it was," Chris said, nodding. "Though . . . I think he's looking for Chestnut and Liz. But from what you said, they're not really horrible people, are they?"

"Well, no . . ." Emily thought about what might happen to them, and to Artie, if they were caught now, just when they were planning to let everything go. "Do you think you could talk to him?"

Chris sighed. "It's asking a lot, but maybe I can convince him to focus his efforts elsewhere. Big Dog might be a good place to start."

It wasn't long before they'd made it up the mountain and pulled into the lane that led to the gates of the Steins' driveway.

Emily, Brandon, and Ana all cheered when Chris parked next to another car. Finally they'd made it, and they were all still together and in one piece.

The music was thumping, and they could see the crowds of people through the huge glass windows, as well as groups hanging out in the driveway, or making their way around the back of the house where there was a full Japanese garden, gazebo, and an infinity pool. The house itself was a minimalist modernist's dream, with steel and glass and sparkling white and black. It looked like something out of an architecture magazine, and with the party going on it was like something from a movie.

"Where are we going to change?" Ana squealed as she stepped out of the car. "There's totally no time for a shower anymore. I have to find Madison." She rushed toward the house with Brandon trailing behind her, Pickles in one hand and her party suitcase in the other.

"So any development between those two?" Chris asked.

Emily just shook her head and smiled. "I don't think they've realized it, but they're totally getting back together. And this time, I completely support the decision."

"What about you? Do you have to go off and change?"

Emily looked down at her jeans and T-shirt and knew she should change or she'd never hear the end of it from Ana, but there was something she had to do first. She'd started the day vacillating about her relationship with Kyle and she hadn't forgotten all of the texts and e-mails he'd sent her throughout the day. But now that she'd finally made a decision—that he wasn't the right guy for her—she had to let him know. *Before* anything happened with Chris.

"There's someone I have to talk to first," she said as she led Chris to the glass double doors at the front of the house. "It's important."

"Don't tell me," Chris said. "You have to speak to a man about some black-market organs you've got to get rid of, before the Colombian government blows your cover." He only seemed to be half joking.

"Close," Emily said. "Old boyfriend."

"Ahh." Chris nodded. "How old?"

"Breakup was recent, but the relationship ended a while ago."

Inside the house Madison seemed to appear from nowhere, her blond hair twisted and pulled to one side to show off a silvery, shimmering tank over a black skirt.

"Emily!" She leaned in and kissed Emily on each cheek. *"Ma chère, ça va bien, non?"* Madison often seemed to be under the impression that she was a French native, especially when she'd had a few drinks.

"Well, thanks. You look amazing, by the way."

"Ah, merci beaucoup!" She looked at Chris and smiled. "And who is this delightful date?"

"Oh, uh . . ." Emily stuttered, not sure what to do about Madison's choice of words. "This is Chris. We're not . . . like . . . we just met, I guess."

"Emily!" Madison wiggled her eyebrows. *"Ooh la la!"*

"It's really not—"

"No need to explain," Madison gushed. "Anyway, come, come. Let's get you some bubbly."

"Actually, I was looking for Kyle."

Madison paused for a moment, then said, "I think I last saw him out by the pool, which is just *parfait* because that's where the champagne is." She took Emily's hand and started pulling her along.

"Champagne at a high-school party?" Chris asked as they made their way through the house. "Things have definitely changed since I graduated two years ago."

"The Steins are a special case," Emily told him. "As I'm sure you can tell."

Out on the patio, things looked even more glorious, like something straight out of a high-quality and high-cost music video. The DJ, whom Emily recognized from her history class, had a full table set up with equipment that Emily couldn't even name, and he was pumping original remixes of the latest songs from his huge speakers.

The infinity pool, which looked amazing even on the absolute worst days, was glowing from the lights inside, and disappeared into the distance, opening out to a view of the tree-covered mountains. People stood all around the patio, laughing, dancing, and drinking the night away.

"For you," Madison said as she handed a tall glass filled with white bubbling champagne to Emily. "And for the *monsieur*." She handed Chris a cold beer. "Kyle should be . . . *ah, voilà!*"

Emily turned to see Kyle making his way over to them. He had on his usual—dark jeans and a fitted henley—and he didn't look bad. But he always looked good, or at least acceptable, and looks weren't the most important part of a relationship. Emily knew she wanted more than that.

"Hey," he said when he was close enough. He nodded at Madison, who quickly twirled around, singing loudly in French at some of her friends who she'd just spotted. "So . . . I hadn't heard from you today. Just saw Brandon and he said your day was kind of fucked up."

"Yeah, well . . ." Emily glanced at Chris, not sure what to do about his presence.

"How about I take a walk around," Chris said. "Maybe I'll track down Brandon and Ana."

Emily let out a breath she hadn't realized she'd been holding. "That'd be great."

Before he walked away, Chris leaned in and gently kissed her cheek. Emily wasn't sure if he'd done it in some effort to show up Kyle, or if he just wanted to do it at that moment, but whatever the reason, she didn't mind.

Once Chris was gone, she turned to Kyle, who was staring at her with wide eyes.

"Why the hell did that guy just kiss you?"

chapter 25

"Really," Kyle said again. "What's going on?"

"Look, Kyle." Emily had never done a breakup before, and she wished she could just play a couple songs to get the point across to him, but that wasn't going to cut it. "We don't work. You know it and I know it. And I think it's time we both accept it."

"But we can make it work," Kyle said quickly. "I can be better. You can be better. Right?"

Emily frowned and shook her head. "What is that supposed to mean?"

"Oh, you know," Kyle stuttered. "We could go out more. You could, I don't know, be less . . . *uptight* about things."

"If by things you mean your pot smoking, then—"

"It's barely a drug," Kyle said quickly. "Everyone does it."

"I don't care, Kyle."

"If you'd just chill out a little . . ."

"That's the thing." Emily took a deep breath. "I shouldn't have to chill out. I'm fine the way I am. And you should find a girl who does want to chill out, just like you. I'm not that girl, and I'll never be that girl. I don't want to be that girl. And

I think when you really consider everything, when you think about it, you'll realize that I'm right."

Kyle was quiet for a moment, then he sighed. "I guess you're right. But don't you think you could've waited before finding some other guy to flaunt in front of me." He motioned in the direction Chris had walked. "I mean, he looks like some kind of biker dude you found at a bar."

"Pool hall."

"Huh?"

"Nothing. It's just been a crazy day."

Kyle crossed his arms, his eyes narrowed at her, but then he nodded. "Okay. Okay, I guess this is the right thing. But we can still be friends, right? I mean, even if this"—he motioned between them—"isn't working out, you're still a cool chick."

"And you're a cool dude," Emily said honestly. "Of course we can be friends."

"Hug it out?"

Emily leaned in and gave Kyle a tight hug. For a second she worried that it'd be a mistake, but he backed away without incident.

"Dude."

Emily frowned. "Look, we can be friends, but when you start calling me dude, then—"

"No, no, not you," Kyle said. "I'm talking about the mad fucking muscle that just strolled in here."

Emily turned around and gawked when she saw who he was referring to. Ruff and Scrappy were at the party, moving through the house with Big Dog right behind them. They'd already spotted her and were coming her way, and she barely had time to comprehend what was happening before they were standing in front of her. Big Dog was grinning.

"Well, hello, *Liz*," he sneered.

"Emily?" Kyle sounded confused, but he also stepped forward, moving slightly in front of her. "There a problem here?"

"Oh, *Emily*." Big Dog nodded enthusiastically. "So nice to finally know your name."

"Hey, dickwad," Kyle said as he stepped up to Big Dog and puffed out his chest. "I don't know who the hell you are, but you can fuck off." He immediately took a step back when Big Dog pulled out a gun and held it right at his chest. "Oh . . ."

"I suggest you reevaluate your tone," Big Dog said slowly. "I'd hate to make a mess on this fancy-ass tile you've got here."

"Look, just leave him alone," Emily said, surprised by the strength in her own voice. She'd expected herself to be scared, and she had been for a moment, but after the day she'd had, she was tired of the nonsense. "What do you want?"

"What do I want?" Big Dog laughed. "What do I *want*?" He pushed Kyle aside and grabbed Emily by the arm. She tried to brace herself, but stumbled and fell toward Big Dog, who spun her around into Scrappy.

Emily felt Scrappy wrap his tree trunk of an arm across her, pinning her against his torso. She couldn't move her arms.

"I'll tell you what I want from you, *Emily*." Big Dog leaned in so close she could feel his warm breath against her cheek, and clearly see the capillaries lacing the edge of the scar across his face. "What I *want* is the one hundred fifty thousand dollars you stole from me today."

Kyle made a move toward them, but Ruff stepped forward and shook his head. Kyle shrank back.

"What's he talking about, Em?"

"I didn't steal anything from you," Emily said. Her voice was shaky now. She'd only had a gun pointed at her once before, and that was several hours prior at Rick's. That gun she found out later had not been loaded. This gun *was* loaded, or was likely to be loaded. It wasn't something she wanted to test. "Liz and Chestnut—the *real* Liz and Chestnut—have the money. We gave it back to them. They're probably trying to get it to you right now." She really hoped she hadn't just sold out the couple by saying that.

"Oh, did you?" Big Dog had a strange smile on his face. "That's really very interesting, *Emily*, because I just caught up with Liz and Chestnut myself, and they informed me that you and your little friends tricked them."

"That had to be before we gave it back." Emily hated the desperate tone in her voice. "We gave them the money. They have it. It wasn't that long ago. Just call them and ask about it. They'll tell you what happened."

Big Dog's eyes flashed fire, but his voice was cold as ice. "If you think for one moment that I'm leaving here without my money, you're wrong. I will pull your fingers off with pliers one by one until you hand it over, and then—"

Emily never heard what Big Dog had planned after he removed her fingers because Kyle lunged around Ruff and tried to swing at Big Dog. His swinging was wild enough to make Scrappy loosen his grip, which gave Emily the chance to pull away, but not before she slammed a foot down on his, crushing his toes with the heel of her boot.

Emily grabbed for Kyle's arm, but as she did, Big Dog regained his footing, and as Ruff was trying to subdue Kyle, Emily saw Big Dog raise the gun by its barrel and bring the butt down hard on Kyle's head. Kyle wilted into Ruff.

By now they'd drawn enough attention that everyone was watching, though no one was doing anything, and it was pretty obvious that they had no idea what to do. Especially once Big Dog had the gun raised and pointed at Emily once again.

chapter 26

The area cleared out, and Emily took several steps back as Big Dog came forward, still grinning.

"Now what?" he asked. "You don't have anyone to save you anymore?"

"Guess again!"

Emily watched as Brandon sprinted from inside the house and tackled Big Dog, and they both hit the ground hard. Ana came running out a moment later, making her way to Emily, but she was quickly swept up by Scrappy. She let out an ear-piercing scream, and at the same time Pickles leaped to her rescue and bit Scrappy's hand, which meant Ana was free but Pickles was now captured.

After a second of scrambling, Emily, Ana, and a bruised Brandon ended up on one side of the pool, while Big Dog, Scrappy, and Ruff were on the other side. Big Dog was holding Pickles in one hand, and his gun in the other.

"Looks like we've got a little problem," he said, holding up the small Chihuahua, who was now shaking with fear.

"Don't you dare hurt my dog, *mulo!*" Ana screamed. Emily

grabbed her arm, since she wasn't sure Ana wouldn't launch herself across the pool to attack.

"Give me my money," Big Dog said. "Or you can kiss your little dog good-bye."

"We don't have it," Brandon said. "Seriously!"

"I tried to tell them." Emily wasn't sure if Big Dog would really shoot a small dog, but she couldn't take the chance. "Just call Liz and Chestnut. They'll get you the money, we promise."

"Your promises don't mean much."

"Don't you think we'd give it to you know if we had it? We don't!" Out of the corner of her eye, Emily saw Chris sneaking closer and closer to Big Dog and his thugs. She didn't know what he could do to help the situation, but it had to be more than whatever they were doing now. She just had to keep them sufficiently distracted. "We were planning to bring the money back to you," she lied. "We got it from Balducci's, and we were going to give it back, but then we met up with Liz and Chestnut, and since they were going to do the job originally, we traded off. They have it."

"And you expect me to believe that you are all okay walking away with nothing?" He laughed. "I'm not an idiot."

"We just want the dog," Brandon said. "That's it."

Chris launched himself forward then, completely surprising Ruff and Scrappy as he tumbled into Big Dog. When they hit the ground, the gun went skidding across the white concrete and Pickles flew through the air and landed in the pool.

Ana let out a banshee-style scream and jumped into the pool, party clothes and all. Brandon immediately followed.

Emily was about to make her way to the other side of the pool to help Chris, who was about to be pulverized as Ruff, Scrappy, and Big Dog all loomed over him, when a loud warrior roar echoed around the patio and four people came rushing from the bushes and trees right toward Big Dog, Ruff, and Scrappy.

Emily's jaw dropped when she saw that it was Buck, Blanche, Chestnut, and Liz.

"Tie them up!" Buck sounded, his voice booming.

It wasn't long before Ruff, Scrappy, and Big Dog were all tied up with rope that Liz had brought in a bag. Chris was now on his feet, gun in hand, breathing hard as he pointed it toward the people who had been about to attack him.

"What the hell?" Brandon said as he got out of the pool, then reached back to pull Ana and Pickles out. "How . . ."

"We're here to apologize," Liz said as she stretched and took a look around at their surroundings. "Nice place."

"*Merci.*" Madison's tiny voice came from somewhere behind Emily.

"This was partially our fault," Chestnut said. "If we hadn't gotten you kids involved at the start of this day, then you would've made it to your party without a hitch."

"When we stopped at the pool hall and figured out what had gone down," Liz said, "and that Big Dog and his cronies were already on their way to finding you, we knew we had to do something to help. There was no way you kids were prepared for these three." She kicked Ruff in the side, and he groaned. "Chestnut called up his parents and we all came right away."

"But how'd you find us?" Ana asked. She motioned at Big Dog. "How'd *he* find us?"

"The bright lights in the sky aren't exactly subtle," Blanche said. "We knew you were headed for a party, and that you were going in this direction. After that it was a guess, but a pretty good one I'd say."

Emily couldn't believe what had just happened, but she also couldn't be more thankful. She rushed forward and threw her arms around Liz and Blanche. Neither woman was the *best* role model, but they were both strong and assertive and knew what they wanted, and Emily could see the good in that.

"Thank you," Emily said. "Really. You didn't *have* to help us, but I'm glad you did." She took a step back and looked down at the criminals tied up at her feet. "Now we just have to decide what to do with these three."

"I got it," Chris said, waving his phone. He quickly dialed, then turned away as he spoke to someone on the line.

Emily and Ana, who was still snuggling Pickles, stood to the side while the others wrangled the tied-up criminals to their feet and began directing them across the patio, and then through the house to the front.

"Okay, everyone!" Madison called out as she strolled around the pool. "I really hope you enjoyed the little show. *C était fantastique, non? Bravo!*" Then as everyone started to relax and talk again, and the music was turned back up, she rushed to Emily and Ana, her eyes wide. "What was *that*?"

"It's . . . complicated," Emily said.

"That's an understatement," Ana said with a laugh.

"We're so sorry, Madison. We'll totally make it up to you."

"I just wish you'd told me," Madison said. "I mean, I love a little *pièce de théâtre* as much as anyone, but I would've set the scene a little better. You know, an introduction. And I would've *volunteered* to be held captive instead of this *petit chien*." She scratched Pickles's head and smiled. "We should get together to plan the next time. Anyway, enjoy the party!" She twirled away, calling out for another glass of champagne.

"She totally thinks we did all of that just to add some excitement to her party, doesn't she," Ana said, incredulous.

Emily nodded slowly, wondering how much champagne Madison had consumed.

"Come on."

Ana took Emily's hand and they walked through the house, fielding lots of questions, and some congratulations, about what had just occurred out by the pool. Emily couldn't believe so many people were taking it in stride. A lot of them seemed to be under the impression, like Madison, that it was all some kind of show she and the others had put together.

That strange setup was apparently easier to comprehend than the reality.

Out in front of the house in the driveway, Big Dog, Ruff, and Scrappy were still tied up, and the others were standing around.

"What's the plan, then?" Emily asked, looking at everyone. "Please tell me there's an actually plan this time. A good one."

"Don't worry," Chris said as he stepped forward. "I called my uncle, and he's sending some cruisers up here to take them away."

"Police!" Chestnut looked around, ready to sprint. "You can't call the police here."

"Wait," Chris said quickly before everyone could explode. "It's okay. He's sending people for them," he pointed to Big Dog and his cronies. "That's it."

Emily wasn't sure whether to ask, but Liz beat her to it.

"What about the . . . money," she asked. "Isn't that going to come up?"

Chris shrugged. "Who's going to believe a trio of drug dealers, and possible smugglers, who just showed up at a high-school party with a gun and threatened the life of some kids."

"And knocked one out!"

Emily glanced back to see Kyle standing in the doorway, obviously fascinated by the scene unfolding, but opting to stay farther away this time.

"You can do whatever you want with that money," Chris continued. "No one will know the difference."

"You can start your cake shop," Ana said.

Liz beamed, and Blanche and Buck looked at her with surprise.

As she crossed her arms, Emily grinned. She could see in Liz's face, and Chestnut's, that they really would be done with their life of crime now. They had enough for Chestnut's classes, Liz's shop, and could probably start a college fund for Artie, not that the kid would have any trouble getting scholarships. Their lives were going to be on track.

Emily just hoped her own life would follow suit.

chapter 27

Chris and Emily stood on the steps and watched as the tail-lights disappeared down the Steins' driveway. The police had taken Big Dog, Ruff, and Scrappy away in separate cars, and Buck, Blanche, Liz, and Chestnut drove off as well.

Back inside, Emily, Ana, and Brandon collapsed together on a couch. Smiling, Chris perched himself on the arm.

"That day was . . ." Brandon sighed, then grinned. "That day was fucking incredible."

Emily let out a burst of laughter. It was insane, sure, but in retrospect . . . the day was kind of awesome. The definition of YOLO.

"We did get Pickles out of it," Ana said, holding up her new dog.

"But can we make a deal?" Emily asked. "Next time we go on any kind of road trip, can we promise *not* to make any stops along the way. Who knows what kind of luck we'll have next time."

"Deal," Ana and Brandon said.

"Aren't you guys pumped for the party?" Chris asked. "That's what this whole thing was about, right?"

Emily nodded as she sank back into the extremely soft, extremely comfortable couch. "Yeah, I suppose . . ." The music thumping from the patio sounded more and more distant by the second. "I'm sure we'll party in a few minutes."

"A few minutes," Ana agreed with a yawn.

Brandon let out a snore in response.

Emily tried to let out a laugh, but at that point exhaustion had taken over. She felt herself slipping into a deep sleep. It'd be a long day. The party could wait.

about the author

Sam Jones has been on several one-day road trips, loves a good party, has never robbed a convenience store, and does not have a pet Chihuahua.

READ ON FOR
EVEN MORE INSANITY IN

JIMMY
October 17, 9:07 P.M.

The eyes were beautiful.

They were mad huge, anime-hero huge, staring out of the darkness.

Something brushed his cheek too, rhythmically. Like kisses.

Jimmy smiled.

Kisses happened all the time to guys like Cam, who expected them. Never to Jimmy.

So he would always remember that moment, how weirdly tender and exciting it was on that deserted road on that rainy October evening, before he blinked and realized his world had gone to shit.

9:08 p.m.

It wasn't the taste of blood that brought him to reality. Or the rain pelting his face through the jagged shark-jaw where the windshield had been. Or the car engine, screaming like a vacuum cleaner on steroids. Or the glass in his teeth.

It was the sight of Cam's feet.

They were thick, forceful feet, Sasquatch feet whose size you knew because Cam bragged about it all the time (14EE), feet that seemed to be their own form of animal life. But right now, in a pool of dim light just below the passenger seat, they looked weightless and demure, curved like a ballerina's. One flip-flop had fallen off, but both legs were moving listlessly with the rhythm of the black mass that lay across the top half of Cam's body—the mass that was attached to the eyes that were staring up at Jimmy.

"Shit!"

Jimmy lurched away. The animal was twitching, smacking its nose against his right arm now, flinging something foamy and warm all over the car. It was half in and half out, its hindquarters resting on the frame of the busted windshield, its haunches reaching out over the hood. The broken remains of a mounted handheld GPS device hung from the dash like an incompletely yanked tooth.

For a moment he imagined he was home, head down on his desk, his mom nudging him awake with a cup of hot cocoa. It was Friday night. He was always home on Friday night. But this was real, and he remembered now—the deer springing out of the darkness, running across the road, legs pumping, neck strained. . . .

"CAAAAAM! BYRON!"

His voice sounded dull, muffled by the rain's ratatatting on the roof. No one answered. Not Byron in the backseat.

Not Cam.

Cam.

Was he alive? He wasn't crying out. Wasn't saying a thing.

Jimmy fumbled for the door handle. His fingers were cold and numb. With each movement the engine screamed, and he realized his right foot was stuck against the accelerator, trapped between it and a collapsed dashboard. He tried to pull it out and squeeze the door handle, but both were stuck. He gave up on his foot and looked for the lock.

There.

The door fell open with a metallic *grrrrrock*. Jimmy hung on to the armrest, swinging out with the door, as a red pickup sped by. It swerved to avoid him, and Jimmy tried to shout for help. His foot still stuck, he spilled out headfirst, twisting so his shoulders hit the pavement. As his teeth snapped shut, blood oozed over his bottom lip. He spat tiny glass particles.

The pickup was racing away, past a distant streetlight, which cast everything in a dim, smoky glow. From the car's windshield, the deer's hind legs kicked desperately in silhouette, like the arms of a skinny cheerleader pumping a victory gesture.

As Jimmy yanked his own leg, not caring if the fucking thing came off at the ankle, he felt the rain washing away the blood. Through the downpour he could see the long, furry face on the seat—nodding, nodding, as if in sympathy. *That's it, pal. Go. Go. Go.*

His ankle pulled loose, and he tumbled backward onto the road, legs arcing over his head. As he lay still, catching his breath, he heard someone laugh, a desperate, high-pitched sound piercing the rain's din.

It took a moment before he realized it was his own voice.

9:09 p.m.

"Jesus, it's still alive!"

Byron's voice. From the backseat.

Byron was okay.

Jimmy jumped up from the road. He struggled to keep upright, his leg numb. He spat his mouth clean as he made his way around the car. Through the side window he could see Byron's silhouette, peering over the front seat. Jimmy looked through the driver's side window. The deer's back was enormous, matted with blood and flecks of windshield. Under it he could make out only the right side of Cam's body from the shoulder down, but not his face.

Cam was completely smothered.

"Oh God, Jimmy, what did you do?" Byron said.

"I—I don't know. . . . It just, like, *appeared!*" Jimmy had to grip the side of the car to keep from falling, or flying away, or completely disintegrating. He blinked, trying desperately to find the right angle, hoping to see a sign that Cam was alive. "Push it, Byron—push it off!"

"It's a monster—how the fuck am I supposed to push it? *Shit, Jimmy, how could you have not seen it?*"

"*I did!*" Jimmy screamed. "I braked. I tried to get out of the way—"

"Dickwad! You tried to outmaneuver a *deer*? You don't *brake*! That makes the grill drop lower—lifts the animal right up into the car, like a fucking spoon! You just *drive*. That way you smack it right back into the woods."

"*If you know so much, why weren't you driving?*"

"With what license?"

"*I don't have one either!*"

"You told me you did!"

"I never told you that! I just said I knew how to drive. I never took the test—"

"Oh, great—the only person in Manhattan our age who knows how to drive, *and you don't bother to get a license.*" Byron leaned closer, suddenly looking concerned. "Jesus Christ, what happened to your mouth?"

"It's what I get for applying lipstick without a mirror—"

"Awwww, *shit!*" Byron was looking at something in his hand. "My BlackBerry's totaled."

"*How can you think about your BlackBerry while Cam is under the deer?*"

Byron looked up with a start, then immediately leaped out of the car. "Oh fuck, Cam. Is he dead?"

"*'Oh fuck, Cam'*? You just noticed him? You're yelling at me, and you just thought of Cam?" Jimmy's hands trembled as he pulled his cell phone out of his pocket. "I'm calling nine-one-one."

"No, don't!" Byron said, snatching the phone from Jimmy's hand.

"*Are you crazy?*" Jimmy said. "What's wrong with you?"

"We're in East Dogshit and the GPS is busted—do you even know what road we're on? What are you going to tell the cops? *Um, there's this tree? And, like, a ditch? And a road?* And then what, we wait? We don't have time, Jimmy!"

"But—"

"Think it through, Einstein. What's your story? One, you wrecked a car that's not yours. Two, you don't have a license. Three, you killed a deer. And four, look at Cam. You planning to go to Princeton and room with Rhodes scholars? How about a guy with three teeth who can't wait for you to bend over? Because if we don't stop talking, dude, you're facing murder charges."

"*He's not dead, Byron—*"

"Just put the fucking phone away and let's get Bambi off Cam." Byron threw Jimmy the phone and raced to the back of the car. "Throw me the keys. I'll get a rope out of the trunk. When I give you back the keys, get in the car."

Jimmy reached into the car, tossing the phone onto the

dashboard. Quickly removing the keys from the steering column, he threw them to Byron. He eyed the driver's seat. The deer was still moving, still trying to get away. *No way* was he going back in there.

But he couldn't abandon Cam.

If only he could think straight. His brain was useless. In that moment, he was picturing a cloud of small, hungry ticks hovering over the front seat. He tried to shake it off, but it was like some weird psychological hijacking brought on by his mother's lifelong vigil over the mortal threat posed by proximity to deer, which turned every suburban outing into a preparation for war.

"What are you fucking worried about, Lyme's disease?" Byron shouted. "Get in there!"

Jimmy cringed. "It's *Lyme*," he muttered, grabbing the door handle. "Not *Lyme's*."

"What?" Byron shouted.

"Nothing. What am I supposed to do—in the car?"

"What the fuck do you think you're supposed to do?"

As if in response, the deer gave a sudden shudder. Jimmy jumped back, stifling a scream. "I—I'm not sure . . ."

"When I give the word, put it in reverse, Jimmy. And gun it."

Byron yanked open the trunk and threw the keys to Jimmy, who kept a wary eye on the deer as he opened the door. It was motionless now, its snout resting just below the gear shift.

As Jimmy climbed inside, the car rocked with Byron's efforts to shove stuff under the rear tires for traction.

Breathe in. Breathe out.

Jimmy tried to stop himself from hyperventilating. He eyed Cam's feet, blinking back tears. He had never liked Cam, or any of the smart-ass jocks who treated the Speech Team kids like they were some kind of lower life-form. Since freshman year he had devoted a lot of time conjuring horrible fates for most of them, fates not unlike this.

In ... Out ...

Jimmy hadn't wanted to go on this drive. It was Byron who'd pushed the idea. *Cam* wants us to go, *Cam* says suburban parties are the best ever, *Cam* says Westchester chicks are hot for NYC guys. *Cam* wants to be friends. It would be stupid to miss a chance at détente between the worlds of sports and geekdom.

In ...

Until this time, Jimmy couldn't imagine that Byron would be friends with a guy like Cam. Byron the potty-mouthed genius, Cam the football guy. Was this some kind of crush? Was *that* the reason for—

"Wake up, douche bag!" Byron shouted. "Now! *Go!*"

With his foot on the brake, Jimmy threw the car in reverse. The accelerator was touching the bottom of the caved-in dashboard. Carefully, he wedged his foot in and floored it.

The engine roared to life, the tires gripping the debris. As the car lurched backward, the deer's head rose slowly off the seat with the force of the rope. Something warm spattered against the side of Jimmy's face.

"AAAGHH!" he screamed, yanking his foot away from the accelerator.

"*WHAT?*" Byron cried, running around the side of the car. "Why'd you stop? We almost had it!"

"*It puked on me!*"

Byron shone a flashlight into the front seat. "It's not puke. It's blood."

"Oh, great . . ." Jimmy's stomach flipped. *This couldn't be happening!*

"Here. This'll protect you." Byron was throwing something over the animal's head—a rag, a blanket, it was impossible to see. "Don't think about it, Jimmy. Just step on it! And put on your seat belt."

Jimmy felt a lightness in his head. His eyes were crossing. *Focus.*

He buckled his belt and put the car in reverse again, slipping his foot under the wreckage of the dashboard. As he floored it, the car began to move, the engine roaring. The animal's hulk rose up beside him, away from him—scraping across the bottom of the windshield, slowly receding out of the car and onto the hood.

The blanket fell off the deer's head, as the carcass finally slipped off, the car jerked backward.

SMMMMACK!

Jimmy's head whipped against the headrest. He bounced back, his chest catching the seat belt and knocking the wind out of him.

"Are you okay?" Byron cried.

"Fah—fah—" Everything was white. Jimmy struggled to breathe, his eyes slowly focusing on the image in the rearview mirror, the twisted metal of a guardrail reflecting against the taillights.

Byron was leaning in the open passenger window, training a flashlight on the dim silhouette of Cam's lifeless body, now freed from the deer. "This does not look good . . . ," he said.

"Is his chest moving?"

"I don't know! I don't think so, but I can't—" In the distance a muffled siren burst through the rain's din. Byron drew back, shutting the flashlight. "Shit! Did you call them?"

"No!" Jimmy said.

"Then how do they know?"

Jimmy thought about the red pickup. "Someone drove past us, just after the accident. Maybe they called."

"Someone saw us?"

"This is a New York suburb. Occasionally people drive on the roads."

"Oh, God. Oh, God. Oh, God. Oh, shit. Oh, God." Byron was backing away from the car, disappearing into the darkness.

"I'm the one who's supposed to be freaking out, not you!" Jimmy

leaned toward Cam's inert body, his hands shaking. The cold rain, evaporating against his body, rose up in smoky wisps. *Don't be dead don't be dead please please please please don't be dead.*

"C-C-Cam?" Jimmy slapped Cam's cheek and shook his massive shoulders, but Cam was limp and unresponsive. His body began to slip on the rain-slicked seat, falling toward the driver's side. Jimmy tried to shove back, but he was helpless against the weight. Cam's head plopped heavily in Jimmy's lap.

"Aaaaghhh!" He pushed open the door, jumped out, and looked around for Byron. "I think he's . . . he's . . ."

The siren's wail was growing closer. How would he explain this? *You see, officer, in New York City no one gets a license until they're in college. But my dad taught me to drive on weekends, on Long Island. No, I don't have the registration either. The car belongs to—belonged to . . . him . . . the deceased.*

He'd have to get out of here before they came. He looked past the car. There was a gully, a hill. It was pitch-black. He could get lost in the night.

Asshole! No, the cops would figure it out. Fingerprints. Friends knew he was driving—Reina Sanchez, she had to know. She was all over Cam. She'd tell them. So it wouldn't only be manslaughter. It would also be leaving the scene of the crime. What was that? Life in prison?

Stay or go, he was screwed either way. Because of a deer. A fucking stupid deer. Without the deer, everything would have been all right.

"BYRON!" he shouted.

In the distance he heard Byron retching, with character-istic heroism.

Cam was now slumped into the driver's seat, his right shoulder touching the bottom of the steering wheel.

He used me. He convinced Byron to get me to drive so he could go to a party. And now he will never ever be accountable. Because he's ...

Dead. He was dead. He would never move again, never talk.

And that opened up several possibilities, some of which were *Unthinkable.*

An idea was taking shape cancerously fast among his battered brain cells. If you were thinking some-thing, it wasn't unthinkable—that was Goethe, or maybe Wittgenstein, or Charlie Brown. The idea danced between the synapses, on the line between survival and absolute awful-ness, presenting itself in a sick, Quentin Tarantino way that made perfect sense.

It was Cam's dad's car. It would be logical that Cam would be driving it.

No one will know.

He grabbed Cam's legs. They were heavy, dead weight. He pulled them across the car toward the driver's side, letting Cam's butt slide with them—across the bench seat, across the pool of animal blood and pebbled glass.

Jimmy lifted Cam into an upright position, but his body fell forward, his torso resting hard against the steering wheel.

HONNNNNNNNNNNK!

The sound was ridiculously loud. Around the bend, distant headlights were making the curtain of rain glow. No time to fix this now.

Jimmy bolted for the woods.

"What are you doing?" Byron called out of the dark. He was standing now, peering into the car. "Jesus Christ! You're trying to *make it look like Cam drove*? What if he's alive? He'll tell them you were driving!"

Jimmy stopped, frantically looking around for something blunt. He stooped to pick up a rusted piece of tailpipe, maybe a foot long. It would do the trick. He knelt by the driver's door and drew it back.

"JIMMY, ARE YOU OUT OF YOUR FUCKING MIND?"

Byron's eyes were like softballs. He grabbed Jimmy's arm.

Jimmy let the tailpipe fall to the ground. He felt his brain whirling, his knees buckling. He felt Byron pulling him away.

As the cop cars squealed to a halt near the blaring car, he was moving fast but feeling nothing.

**HERE'S A LOOK AT A NOVEL
THAT'S SURE TO MAKE YOU SAY,**

"wtf!"

Pre-game

I decided for about the hundredth time tonight that I'm not going to Cassandra Castillo's spring break barter party.

Then I changed my mind, because, fuck it: I'm seventeen, lonely, and horny. If I bailed on the party, not only would Coop and Ben never forgive me, but I'd have nothing else to do tonight that didn't involve a bottle of hand lotion and a crusty sock of Catholic shame.

Friday night. I was sitting in a booth at a greasy dive with my best friends, Coop and Ben, praying for the finger of God to wipe us and the whole stupid town of Rendview off the map so that I wouldn't have to make a decision about Cassie's party. The problem wasn't the party. It was the hostess of the party and the fact that, for the first time since freshman year, she was single. And not just single. Newly single. In fact, she had barely been free of the shackles of monogamy for an entire week. But if I was going to make my move, I couldn't afford to waste time.

Coop interrupted my Cassie-filled daydreams by asking me and Ben a totally irrelevant question. "Who'd play you in a movie about your life?" Coop flashed a grin, unleashing the dimples from which no teenage girl is immune. Which sucks for them because he's totally into dudes. One dude in particular.

Ben snatched a fry off my plate and shoved it into his mouth without so much as a please or thank you. Which is how Ben is. Love him or loathe him, you don't get between him and a french fry. Not if you value your fingers. "Definitely Jake Gyllenhaal," Ben said.

"Just because he plays you," Coop said, "doesn't mean you get to bang him."

"Unless he's a method actor."

"You are pretty good at fucking yourself," I said, and pulled my plate of limp fries out of his reach.

Ben kissed Coop on the cheek and said to me, "You'd be played by a Muppet. And the movie would be called: *Simon Cross and the Blue Balls of Destiny.*" Ben cracked up at his own joke and slid out of the booth to go talk to friends at another table.

Coop, Ben, and I had been best friends since grade school, when we all got stuck at the same lunch table with Phil Bluth. Banding together was the only way to protect our precious pudding cups from Phil's grabby hands. We were the Three Musketeers. The Three Amigos. Peter, Ray, and Egon. Until junior year of high school, when Ben and Coop coupled up. I thought it was great that they had fallen in lust and all that sappy bullshit, but I often felt like the third wheel of a trike that longed to be a big, bad, two-wheeled bicycle, riding off into the sunset, leaving me to pedal solo on the lonely road to Loserville. Population: me.

"Earth to Simon." Coop snapped his fingers in front of my eyes and brought me back to our sticky booth in the middle of Gobbler's, which is famous for being one of the few places in town that won't immediately call the cops on kids for hanging out, and not at all famous for their lousy burgers. Rendview is a sleepy beach town on the east coast of Florida, and there isn't much to do except eat, sleep, surf, and get drunk. That last item was on everyone's agenda for the evening. Gobbler's was wall-to-wall with my classmates. It was the last Friday of spring break and we were all getting ready to migrate to Cassie's house for a night of balls-to-the-wall teenage rebellion.

Despite the fact that I couldn't wait to graduate from the soul-rotting drudgery of high school, I felt a bond with some of these guys, forged from our years of shared suffering. Suffering that would come to an end at our imminent graduation.

"Ben's only messing with you," Coop said.

"I'm a loser," I said. "A seventeen-year-old virgin. I'm going to graduate in a couple of months, go to community college, and end up sleeping with someone like Mrs. Elroy because I repulse girls my own age with my wit and charm and concave chest."

"Don't sell yourself short," Coop said. "Mrs. Elroy was hot back in the nineteen twenties."

"Lucky me." I picked at one of my fries but tossed it down without eating it. "Even if I did manage to bag her, she'd end up showing me the door before I've had a chance to say, 'I swear it doesn't usually happen that fast'—though who am I kidding, it always happens that fast—because her husband will be home any moment and, oh wait, I think that's him now. Better jump out the window. Naked. Yeah, good times."

Coop laughed into his napkin, and I thought for a minute that he was going to choke, which would have served him right. But the bastard had the nerve to cough and catch his breath again. "It's not that dire. There are plenty of girls that'll do you."

"If you say Aja Bourne, I'm going to punch your face off."

"No," Coop said. "We'll find you a nearsighted girl who likes to binge drink."

"I'd prefer something less date-rapey."

"Who's date-raping whom?" Ben asked as he slid back into the booth, throwing his ropey arm around Coop's shoulders. Ben is always in motion, even when he's sitting still. It's like his molecules can't stop bouncing around. Our school had suggested he go on ADHD meds back in eighth grade, but Ben's mom had told them where they could stick their pills. Four years later, Ben is about to graduate with a free ride to MIT. Guess he showed them.

"I'm not date-raping anyone," I said, loudly enough that a couple of kids at the closest tables turned to gawk.

Ben was eyeballing my fries, so I pushed the soggy leftovers across the table. "Maybe more girls would be into you if you weren't so obvious about your Cassie fetish," he said

"Ixnay on the Assie-Cay," Coop said. I hate how he and Ben treat me like a feral monkey who's going to fling his shit at them every time they mention Cassie's name. Sure, I'm totally into the girl, but I'm not obsessed.

"The party is at Cassie's house," I said. "She was going to come up eventually." I did my best to keep my voice even and calm. I'd had plenty of practice.

Here's the lowdown on the Cassie situation: I love her. The feeling isn't, technically, mutual. Maybe, possibly, somewhere deep,

deep down where even she doesn't know they exist, Cassie might have some sweaty feelings for me, but it's highly unlikely. Girls like Cassie don't go for skinny geeks like me, in spite of my awesome hair.

And that should have been the end of it, except that freshman year, I'd done the unthinkable. I'd asked her out. And she'd said yes. We'd gone on one date and I'd nearly kissed her but—

"Are you thinking about mini-golf again?" Ben asked. Without waiting for an answer, he slapped me across the face so hard that spit flew out of my mouth and hit the wall. Someone whispered, "Cat fight," from a nearby table, and hissed.

Coop and I gaped at Ben. "Negative reinforcement," Ben said. "Every time he thinks about, talks about, or looks at Cassie, I'll slap him."

I put my hand to my cheek and wiggled my jaw. "You, sir, are a douchenozzle."

"I could punch you in the balls instead." Ben made a fist and leaned forward.

Coop held Ben back. "Can we save the ball punching for later?"

"Or never," I said.

"But Ben has a point," Coop said. "Just yesterday you were going on and on about how the party is the perfect chance for you to tell Cassie you love her and to finally kiss her, finishing what you started at Pirate Chang's."

Ben gulped some of my soda. "That was years ago, buddy. Time to move on. Your crush, while adorable, is starting to curdle. Pretty soon you're going to be that creepy guy who lives in his parents' basement, wallpapering his bedroom with old pictures of the girl he can't get over."

My friends had a point, but that didn't stop my brain from churning out scenario after scenario—imagined histories of what my life might have been like if I'd kissed Cassie that night instead of letting her get away. I feel about Cassie the way Coop feels about Ben. And even though I know that Cassie doesn't feel the same way about me, I've hoped. For years, every time she talked to me, every time she smiled in my direction, I hoped.

"Let's say you do make a play for Cassie tonight," Coop said. "And, for the record, I'm not saying I think it's a good idea. What about Eli?"

"Don't egg him on," Ben said. "Simon's got as much chance of scoring with Cassie as he has of scoring with me."

"Wow," I said. "Thanks for the support."

"I'm not trying to be a dick—"

"It comes more naturally to some," I said.

"Simon, listen. Cassie is pretty. She's popular. She's smart as shit. She dates guys like Eli Horowitz. Eli Fucking Horowitz, man."

"She dumped him."

Ben chuckled. "Do you honestly believe that means he won't break you into tiny pieces and then break those pieces into even smaller pieces? Look at him."

We all turned to the far corner where Eli sat alone. He looked like reheated dog shit. Like he hadn't shaved since school let out for spring break. Like he hadn't showered or even bothered to put on clean clothes. I was willing to bet the cost of my meal that Eli stank like the insides of my gym shorts. And yet, despite looking like a New York City hobo, he was still built like someone who could and would tear me from crotch to crown. His arms are the size of my thighs and his thighs are the size of my torso. His dusky skin hoarded shadows, making him appear even more dangerous. Which he was. Eli was a wrestling god at Rendview. And an honor student, and homecoming king, and staring at us.

"I could take him," I said, trying to look like I wasn't looking. "Anyway, he's mourning Cassie, not trying to get back with her."

Ben patted my hand. "Simon, I would love nothing more than to see you and Cassie sneak off to a quiet bedroom to fulfill your porniest fantasies so that you can finally move on with your life, but it's never going to happen. Ever. Not in your lifetime or mine. Not in a parallel universe where you and Cassie are the last human specimens on a planet ruled by poodles."

I leaned back in the booth and crossed my arms over my chest. "Your confidence in me is inspiring. No, really, I may weep. Here come the tears."

"Just keeping it real."

"Don't be mean," Coop said.

"Sorry," Ben said, but not to me. He and Coop got those silly looks on their faces that meant they were dangerously close to engaging in some full-frontal smoochery. Thankfully, a tall girl with long blond hair strolled over to our booth and saved me from that ungodly display. We waited for her to say something, but she stood there awkwardly for a long moment.

"Did you forget your lines?" Ben asked.

The girl shook her head. I noticed a long scar that ran along the bottom of her chin. "Ketchup," she said.

"It's not a vegetable, kids."

I kicked Ben under the table. "Don't mind Ben," I said. "He thinks he's funny when he's mostly just an ass." I grabbed the ketchup from the end of the table and passed it to her.

"You're Simon, right?" the girl asked. I nodded. "I'm Natalie Grayson." She smiled brazenly.

Something about that smile reminded me of—"Wait. We had sophomore geometry together, didn't we?"

"Yeah." Natalie's face lit up.

"What did the guy say when he got back from vacation and found his parrot's cage empty?"

"Polly gone," she said, and we both laughed.

Ben groaned and muttered something under his breath that sounded like "geeks," but I ignored him.

"Are you going to Cassie's party?" Natalie asked.

"Totally."

"What's the deal with the bartering thing?"

I'd already made Coop explain it to me a thousand times. I mean, I got the concept but didn't see the point. "You bring stuff to the party," I said. "And you trade it for other stuff."

"Like what?" Natalie stood holding that ketchup bottle with both hands. I was afraid she was going to squeeze a tomato geyser into the air.

Ben reached into his pocket and pulled out a little plastic bag with a dozen white pills in it. "Once people get shit-faced, I'm going to make a mint with these. People will trade me anything for them."

"Drugs? Really?" Natalie did not sound impressed.

"They're baby aspirin." Ben put his finger to his lips and gave the girl one of his patented winks.

"I still don't get why," I said.

"For fun, dumbass. What'd you bring?" Coop asked Natalie.

She looked over at her table, which was packed with girls I knew by sight but not by name. They were the minor-league hitters. Not A- or B-list girls, but not part of the moo crew either. "I stole some tiny liquor bottles from my dad, and I have a guitar pick signed by Damian Crowley of Noodle Revolution."

Ben faked puking into my empty basket of fries. He hates NR. Hates. So much that he started an anti-fan club.

"You can totally trade up with that," Coop said, ignoring Ben's continued mock vomiting. "It's like that Canadian guy who started with a red paperclip and bartered his way up to a house. You could trade your guitar pick for a hot prom date if you played it right."

"Fat chance," Ben muttered, but we all ignored him.

Coop was giving me a look, this mental nudge that he seemed to think I understood. For the record, I did not. But, apparently, I wasn't the only person at the table who didn't get Coop, because Natalie was looking at him like he'd been speaking Parseltongue.

"Maybe I'll see you at the party, Simon," Natalie said, stuttering her way through the sentence, her earlier store of bravery seemingly all used up. "Thanks for the ketchup."

"Anytime," I said. "You need ketchup, I'm your man. Call me Mr. Ketchup. Or, you know, not."

I watched Natalie walk back to her table, where she said something to her friends that made them giggle and squeal.

An idea struck me. "Coop, you're a genius."

"Tell me more," Coop said.

"That thing you said about bartering a paperclip for a house. Was that true?"

"Indeed." Coop grinned at me, and then at Natalie. "You can do anything you want tonight, Simon."

"Then I'm going to barter for a kiss from Cassie. I'm going to tell her that I love her."